THE STONE GATE CLUB MYSTERIES

COULD THERE BE GHOSTS IN
THIS OLD CLUB HOUSE?

JM WHITNEY

authorHOUSE®

AuthorHouse™
1663 Liberty Drive
Bloomington, IN 47403
www.authorhouse.com
Phone: 1 (800) 839-8640

Published by AuthorHouse 05/30/2020

ISBN: 978-1-7283-6337-0 (sc)
ISBN: 978-1-7283-6336-3 (e)

Library of Congress Control Number: 2020910103

THE BEGINNINGS

My name is Mildred Murdock. Most everyone calls me Milly. A while ago, I began writing about a ghost that lived at the Stone Gate, a social club in Knox, Vermont. It started when my husband, Howard, and I entertained some friends at the club for our fortieth wedding anniversary. They were sure that they had encountered a ghost while spending the night in one of the club's guest bedrooms on the second floor. As it was not the first time that I had been alerted to the possibility of a resident ghost, I felt compelled to try to figure out if the stories were true or just in the imaginations of those relating the stories.

Howard and I have been members of the club for a few years. Because we live in an adjacent town, it is easy for us to visit the club frequently. We enjoy the ambiance of the club and the members, who make us feel comfortable and welcome.

As I wrote the main story, I was happy with the way it was evolving, so I kept on adding more stories as I learned of them from club members and staff. Some of the tales come from actual events in this amazing house's history. However, please don't hold me to the facts, as I cannot provide proof for most of the stories that I have heard. Older homes are particularly vulnerable to people suspecting that they might be haunted. As we all have imaginations, it seems natural to expect some folks to be sensitive to unusual happenings when attending an event in an older establishment.

CHAPTER 1

THE HOLIDAYS

The Stone Gate Club is and has been the perfect setting for major celebrations: fun birthday parties, anniversaries, and private events for family members who love and use the club and memorable luncheons and dinners for local organizations and groups that hold their events in this special place. Many a bride has been feted under a large tent on the grounds or inside in the wonderful music room, which is graced by a uniquely carved clay fireplace. Some of the events that Howard and I have attended have begun by us sitting near the fireplace and warming ourselves from the cold outside.

Last year as the holidays approached, with Halloween and then Thanksgiving setting the pace, the club's staff and the members of the decorating committee had been prepared. The club's delicious, annual Thanksgiving dinner was also on the list.

They had busily spread the decorations of the autumn season around the club. Hay bales topped with pumpkins and corn husks sat on the porch. Corn stalks graced the entrance to the club. A lovely arrangement of fall leaves cuddling with asters in gourds graced each dinner table.

The decor contributed as much to the event as the delicious turkey and accompanying dishes, which filled the buffet table. A station for yummy pumpkin, apple, and pecan pies, which were ready to be topped with ice cream, awaited those who could still manage dessert after the sumptuous dinner.

Members, their families, their friends, and special guests arrived in time to have a few cocktails before the meal. As more and more people arrived, the noise in the room became quite loud.

Lila, the bartender, was busy serving mimosas, bloody marys, or other drinks of choice. Lila was working so hard to keep up with the drink orders that later when asked, she said she hadn't noticed the little person sitting under the table where she kept her supply of extras for the bar. Suddenly, there had been a crash. Bottles and glasses were scattered all over the table and the floor. The little person scampered out of hiding, looked around the room, and quickly ran to join her family.

Had anyone noticed her? Oh, yes! The guests who had been waiting for their libations at the bar had wondered about the unusual event—seeing a child in the barroom. Children were not usually allowed in that room.

It turned out that Little Alice Rawley had been scolded by her mother for not being as nice to her aunts as her mom had wanted her to be. While in a pout, Alice had found refuge under the barroom's table. A little bug had tried to land on her while she was sitting under the table sucking her thumb. She suddenly screamed and tried to get out of the bug's way.

Her parents, Jeff and Judy Rawley, were mortified as they felt a change in the moods of the members who had observed the antics of this little six-year-old. Howard and I had watched the events, and we were very surprised at the change in attitude. Alice's grandparents, Scott and Irene Rawley, were embarrassed also. They tried to change the situation by supplying bottles of wine to the dinner tables of those who were involved.

The buffet bell sounded. After a visit to the buffet table, which was loaded with food, everyone sat down with a plate full of the delicious cuisine that Cliff Johnson, the chef, had supplied.

Earlier, we had had a chance to renew friendships as we had arrived and had placed our orders at the bar. We had seen to it that our family members who were new to the club had had a short tour of the downstairs before sitting down to eat.

It was a special moment for Howard and me as we looked across the dinner table at our children, their children, and their children's boyfriends and girlfriends. They had grown up so fast.

Howard had insisted on providing Thanksgiving neckties for the males of the family. I had made bracelets for the females. There was much joking and threatening to remove their neck and wrist adornments if their parents didn't let them be excused every now and then, to check on the football games, which were on the TV in the tavern room.

Once our meal was finished, we realized that it was almost time for our favorite team to begin playing. Our friends, the Kimballs and Charlotte and Earl Springs, joined us as we left the dining room and headed to the Tavern Room.

The Tavern Room was a very warm and comfortable room, which had dark wood paneling. There was a fireplace in the center of the back wall, which was framed by a hearty mantle. Pewter beer steins were displayed on the mantle. Paintings of earlier times in the life of Knox hung above it. The fireplace was aglow. Round tables and chairs were scattered around the room. A big-screened TV covered another wall. For this event, the bar was open and well equipped with the members' favorite beverages.

For the first time, the Springs had decided to have their Thanksgiving dinner at the club. They had been members for a little over a year. It was a real treat for them to be there. They were also entertaining Charlotte's relatives: her Mother, Meg Brown, and two of Meg's sisters, Tammy Green and Phyllis Hill. It was a *first* for them as well. Before the dinner, the ladies had spotted folks in the bar that they had recognized from town. The two women had retired, and they lived together in a lovely condominium in Knox.

One of the first families that they had recognized had been the Kimballs. Kent Kimball always had something wise and witty to say to the rather staid ladies, which would make them a bit embarrassed. He also made them blush when he complimented them or commented on the way that they looked.

Today during cocktail hour in the bar room, he had teased them about the suspected ghost at the club. His comments had been heard by those who had been near him. Some of those people had looked a little surprised and a bit nervous.

Paula and Kent Kimball had been regulars at each Thanksgiving dinner since the year that they had joined the club. Kent was always interested in sports, as he was a retired reporter from *The Washington Post*'s sports' department and followed sports avidly. Paula had become very accustomed to his excitement over each game that he watched, and to be honest, she was also addicted to sports.

Paula, Kent, and their grown-up children, Max and Mildred, took their places at a table near the TV. The two kids had come home from college for the holiday. Max attended Harvard, and Milly was a freshman at Cornell. They had grown up celebrating their holidays at the club. As soon as they found their table and sat down, the channel was changed to ABC, where the football game was beginning.

"What could be better on this Thanksgiving afternoon than a full tummy, a warm fire, and congenial folks gathering together to help cheer on their favorite team?" asked Ralph Martin, the next person that entered the tavern room.

Ralph was a long-standing member of the club. Having served on the board of governors for a few terms, he had recently assumed the role of coordinator for the house committee. Ralph loved the club's events. He was enthusiastically vocal when enjoying sports around the holidays. He was available to help put events together, and he supplied many suggestions on how to operate the club to make it profitable and workable.

As the afternoon progressed, the cheering for the football game grew louder. The bartender was busy filling orders and setting up more seating for latecomers. By the time the game ended, there was no space left in the room.

Howard and Kent, who were two football-loving friends, had taken over the table that was just in front of the TV. I was chatting with Charlotte Spring, when suddenly, there was a crash, which was accompanied by a moan, running steps, and another crash. The room was so crowded that it was almost impossible to know exactly where and what had happened. The noise seemed to come from the bar area.

According to Lila, the bartender, she had filled an order and had placed it on a tray, which had been on the counter. Someone had picked up the glass as if to drink from it, and then had thrown it on the floor. She was so busy that she couldn't remember who the person had been. Her memory was foggy regarding the person's face. She was almost positive that it had been a guest of one of the members, but she couldn't see anyone in the crowd around the bar who had that face.

We heard more running and then another crash. Earl Spring was just about to speak to me, but he shook his head and later told me what had happened.

He said that he was one of the first members to reach the bar. He listened to all that Lila was saying and then turned around and walked to the door that led to the hallway outside of the Tavern Room. As he entered the hall, he thought that he caught sight of someone just closing the door at the end of the staircase that led to the second floor. As he reached for the doorknob, it fell onto the floor. He was not able to open the door without a doorknob.

Frustrated, Earl returned to the Tavern Room. By this time, some of the crowd had begun to leave. Reaching his table, he looked back at the bar where Lila stood. Her back was turned to the bar as she tried to clean up the mess on the floor. Earl saw a drink on a tray that was on the bar.

When Lila turned around, she gasped because she now saw a drink on the tray once again. She reached for it, sniffed the glass, and took a sip. It was the same drink that she had put there before. She wondered if someone was playing games with her. Who would have had the temerity to do such a thing when she was so busy trying to keep up with orders?

Being a seasoned employee of the club, Lila worked her head off to accommodate the members so that they might enjoy the club during the holidays. Lila was a very popular figure at all of the club's events throughout the year. She had a memory like a steel trap. She was aware of each person's favorite beverage and was quick to make sure that drink would be available at events where that member would be attending.

The incident didn't impact the guests much. Most of them said farewell and left for home without giving another thought to the events of those last few minutes.

I was at the door of the Tavern Room leading to the hallway and to the rest of the building as the Spring family was leaving. Earl was stopped and looking at a door that led to the second floor with a surprised expression on his face. I watched him as he rushed to the door and put his hand on the knob. It was once again in the hole where it had been earlier. Now he really looked puzzled. By the look on his face, I gathered that he was questioning his own memory of what had happened in the Tavern Room.

Earl returned to the bar area. As he did, he spotted me, turned around, and caught my eye. Howard and I had been talking about his bet on the game. As Earl stared at me, I had to respond. I patted my husband's hand and excused myself. I rushed over to Earl.

As he spoke, I knew that I had not seen anyone pick up the glass and throw it, but I could confirm all the other activity. We moved back into the stairwell, and Earl tested the knob again. The door opened. As he looked at the staircase, he was surprised to find a shard of glass on the second step. He picked it up and said that it felt wet. After sniffing it, he concluded that it had contained an alcoholic drink.

I was just as puzzled as Earl was. I warned him not to throw out the piece of glass just as he was about to toss it into the garbage. At least he didn't think that he had dreamed the incident at the bar, as I was there to confirm his story.

He picked up the shard and put it into his handkerchief. He was careful not to blot out the wetness. We went back to the bar. He told his family to go to the car and that he would join them shortly.

Lila was still working on picking up pieces of broken glass and cleaning the floor around the place where the drink had been thrown. "Do you mind looking at this for me?" asked Earl.

As Lila turned around, I noticed that she looked rather pale. Lila took the piece of glass and saw that it was wet. She sniffed it. She said, "Sure enough, it may have come from the glass that was tossed on the ground."

"Impossible!" Earl said explosively. This was on a staircase behind a closed door. How could it have gotten there without someone putting it there on purpose?"

As Earl looked like he was trying to fathom how the shard of glass had been left on the staircase, he turned to ask Lila another question, however, she slowly fell to the floor. "Lila!" he shouted. He tried to reach her, but he was not quick enough. She had fainted. A drop of blood ran down her face. Her head must have hit a something on her way to the floor.

The folks who were left in the tavern room became so quiet that you might have heard a pin drop. Someone called the paramedics, who arrived about ten minutes later. A quick examination of her head proved the wound to be only a minor one. However, by this time, Lila was complaining of stomach cramps. When she felt a queasiness in her stomach, she rushed to the ladies' room, and she was extremely sick.

Everyone in the tavern room was rattled. How had Lila become so ill that she had fainted? What had happened to Lila that could develop into a problem for the entire club? Was it a bug going around that someone had introduced to the festivities?

With that in mind, the staff raced to the ladies' room, with disinfectants in hand. Then they tackled the bar. The word went out to those members who were still in the tavern to be sure to wash their hands as soon as possible. They were also supposed to report anyone else who might have been infected with whatever Lila had. The warning was clear: *Be alert!*

Earl quickly checked with those members and guests who had remained in the Tavern Room. We were okay. Our family just took what was happening in stride. Our children left and walked outside to enjoy the remains of Thanksgiving with those who were also slowly heading toward their cars and homes.

Earl got into his car and drove his family home. Later, he told me that he tried to explain the events of that last hour to his wife and her relatives. Earl had wondered aloud if there had been any chance that the liquor had been contaminated. Then he and his family had concluded that if that had been the case, the friendly ghost of the Stone Gate Club had done its best to alert members not to drink that brand of booze.

Could that have been the reason for this ugly event? Was a ghost trying to make sure that folks were safe?

LEFTOVERS

The night after Thanksgiving, members again arrived at the club to enjoy the annual leftover dinner night. This dinner had been started a couple of years earlier by a member named Joanie Karlson, who was heading south for the winter the next day and didn't want to cook before leaving her home in the mountains.

Occasionally, the leftover meal was better attended than Thanksgiving dinner was. This year, that was not so. However, everyone had a great time, and the meal was much loved by members who didn't have to cook or serve a meal that night at home after having celebrated the day before. They were tired from all the cooking and entertaining.

During the cocktail hour, Lila, who had recovered from her bout of illness from the day before, was bartender again. Dinner was served shortly after this in buffet style, by the staff. Mary Ann Kingston, the sous chef, had planned the menu well. It consisted of typical leftovers from the Thanksgiving meal: potatoes, turkey, gravy, meatloaf, and other items, some of which added to the tastiness of a Thanksgiving leftover dinner. People were able to pick their favorite combination of foods.

The dinner went smashingly well. Those attending were especially pleased with the desserts, which, of course, meant pumpkin pie, apple pie, and an assortment of other holiday desserts, including the delicious mincemeat cookies, for which Chef Cliff Johnson was famous.

While the guests were helping themselves to the desserts, the cookies disappeared. A trail of crumbs had been left from the buffet room to the men's library. Then it went on into one of the two closets in that room.

The staff was dumbfounded. Nothing like that had ever happened before. Mary Ann investigated the closets and finally found the platter of cookies. She tried to collect the remnants of the cookies so that she could replace them on the dessert table, but she couldn't make it work. The cookies crumbled every time someone picked one up. The platter was removed and taken to the kitchen. It was very discouraging for those guests who really looked forward to the yummy cookies each year.

Mary Ann picked up a cookie to check it out. It crumbled in her hands. *Oh, well*, she thought, *no one will miss this one*. She devoured it. About twenty minutes later, she felt ill and raced for the bathroom.

"Good thing those cookies were not served to the members or we'd have a real issue on our hands," claimed Cliff Johnson, the club manager.

It seems that the cookie dough contained some bug repellant. How it ever found its way into the dough, no one knows. Obviously, someone had been alerted to that fact and had quickly removed the cookies from the dessert table. Was the ghost at work again?

READY SET GO

The Sunday after the Thanksgiving holiday celebration, two very important staff members, Jean and George Rand, arrived at the club. As Jean later told me, they had been recruited by Jennifer Strong, who was head of the entertainment committee, to help prep for the upcoming Christmas events.

I knew that Jean was employed by Chef Cliff Johnson as a staff member who also served members of the club during their dinner events. She said that she had convinced her darling, retired husband to work for Cliff and the club as well, doing some of the things that required a good mind, clear thinking, and some physical strength.

They unlocked the front door, walked into the club, and ascended the main staircase and then the stairs to the third floor where all the club decorations and important historical documents were stored. When they reached the third floor, they found a mess. Decorations for Thanksgiving, Columbus Day, Halloween, new members' night, which had been celebrated the previous September, and Valentine's Day, which had happened earlier in the year, were piled up willy-nilly.

They were astonished that the members had left a mess after each event. Before they could even begin to find decorations for the upcoming Christmas season, they had to sort through and put away all of the items that were in the way.

Finally, they finished putting away the decorations, and they were able to see the boxes that held the Christmas decorations. They found the artificial trees first and took them down to the first level of the club. Next came the boxes and boxes of tree decorations: ribbons, ornaments, bells, and lights. You name it, and it was there.

Bless them for the yeoman's job that they did in finding all those important items for the team of decorators. The next morning, the team would begin the job of dressing up the Stone Gate Club for the holidays. I am sure that Jean and George were exhausted when they were finished.

Jean told me that they were still a bit intrigued with the stories that they had heard from the staff during that week. George asked his wife if she believed that a ghost might have caused all the ruckus. Jean just looked at him. She shrugged her shoulders and then gave him a big smile.

She said, "George, you remember the incident that I told you about last spring. It was the time when the club door was locked and Cliff arrived to cook for Easter. He couldn't open it for love or money. Then suddenly, it was unlocked, and it opened. We staff members wondered if the ghost of the club might have been tricking him."

George just looked at her, gave her a big smile, and said, "No comment."

Early the next morning (a bit too early for some of us), Howard and I arrived to be part of the decorating team. Jennifer Strong, our boss who was also chairman of the entertainment committee, arrived with the other members of the team, who were at the club to make honey out of lemons with the decorations for the Christmas holidays and upcoming events at the club.

We sifted through many boxes. It proved to be an awesome task. By noon, some of the group members were ready to quit, but others arrived to take their places. Three days later, Jen Strong and her team were very pleased. The club looked like it should during the holidays. Trees were in place, decorated, and lighted. Strings of lights adorned the porch and other special places. Each room had a special theme, and the decorations reflected that theme. The club looked like a fairyland of holiday spirit.

Jen congratulated the team members, who were surprised at how much work had gone into the job and yet how wonderful the atmosphere had become. It made the work we had done seem like nothing compared to the pride we had in a job well done.

The evening that the entertainment committee had chosen for the celebration of Christmas arrived. The carolers who had been hired arrived on time, dressed in their wonderful old-fashioned costumes. They began singing the great tunes of the holiday season as they strolled up and down the porch.

As a member of the entertainment committee, I was responsible for the program that evening. I had asked Howard to come early to this wonderful event and made sure that all of my plans were in place.

As each family arrived and walked onto the porch, I was aware that the floor squeaked. The noise went unnoticed by those were traveling to the front door. However, the carolers heard the noise. They called me over to ask if they could move indoors to complete their singing.

By that time, most of the guests had arrived, and they were involved in conversations with friends while enjoying their cocktails in the bar room. The Carolers moved indoors. They took up a position at the foot of the formal stairway to the second floor. They Continued their wonderful renditions of Christmas carols.

Howard and I urged members to join in the singing. When they joined in the singing, the club rang with the spirit of Christmas and contributed to the magical atmosphere of the holidays.

As more people arrived for the evening and approached the front door, there was a loud rumble. One of the members, Scott Rawley, had just arrived. He was standing at the doorway of the club. He spotted his wife Irene and rushed over to her. He looked like he was worried that something might harm her. They were puzzled at what might have happened to cause such a noise on the porch.

Some folks went to the door to find out what was happening and to see what the noise was all about. While looking up from the lawn on the croquet court, they could see that a massive section of the roof over the top of the porch contained an enormous amount of snow. This was not a surprise because the week prior to this evening's event had brought snow daily. However, the snow had decided to slide off the roof that evening.

The noise was horrific, making the observers run for cover inside the club. All escaped, and no one was hurt. They were just a bit afraid when they saw the massive amount of snow come down. After everyone had calmed down, the questions came. Why had it happened?

"Didn't the club clean off the roof over the front door after the storm," Howard asked, "especially when there was a pending event?" I shrugged my shoulders. I had no answer to that question.

As conversations continued, members, who had been at the front door, said that they had observed a strong wind. It must have blown the snow off the roof. It had blown the snow from the front porch across the lawn of the croquet court and then into the woods beyond. There hadn't been any wind anywhere else but only behind the snow falling from the roof.

As I looked at the front of the club's building where the snow had come from, there was a very dim light and a figure moving along the edge of the roof. It was there, and then it was gone. Then I noticed new members Naomi Wilson and her husband Randy on the porch. They had just arrived as the snow had fallen off the roof. They had seen it blow across the croquet court.

Naomi told me later that the members who had been standing nearby had seemed to shrug off the incident. She said that they had seemed to attribute it to another event of the season and had moved into the bar to collect their drinks.

Naomi also said that she was a bit shaken by the whole incident. She told me that she didn't want to show her nervousness, as she and Randy were new members of the club and wanted to make a good impression. That is one reason why Naomi had asked Randy to attend that evening's Christmas-caroling event—to get to know the other members and to make a good impression.

She told me that they were newcomers to Knox and the music world of the mountains. Randy had been working at the Met in New York City for the past ten years as a tenor in its esteemed opera company. Now he wanted to become involved with Snaglewood Music Center productions and the Lyric Opera Company of the Mountains. He was ready to retire from the hectic pace of New York City. Naomi was delighted that Randy had made these decisions, as she was a big fan of the area and always had been.

Naomi was Randy's second wife. They had met when she, as an usherette, had been asked to deliver a message to Randy backstage. She had never even seen backstage at the Met. She felt a mild panic while trying to deliver the message to Randy's dressing room.

She said that Randy was in a rush to answer the stage call for his rehearsal. He was coming out the door of his dressing room and wasn't looking around him. The door slammed right in Naomi's face. She went down with a crash. She said that Randy seemed to be mortified. He tried to help her up, but she was bleeding so profusely that she couldn't see who was there, and she refused the help. Randy reached down and picked her up. She was as light as a feather. He carried her into the first-aid station nearby and settled her on the examining table. After a quick look around, he spotted some sanitary wipes in a jar, which hung on the wall near the table. He grabbed a couple of them and gently wiped the blood off Naomi's face.

She was so startled that she almost slapped his hand away. Then she realized that he was just trying to help her and that he was being nice. She decided to smile at him instead and to say, "Oh, thanks."

Naomi said that she was aware of how interested he seemed as he cleaned up her face. He looked surprised as he gazed at her. He told her later that he had discovered the most wonderful green eyes that he had ever seen, then her lovely lips, and then her red hair. "Wow!" he told her, "I thought I sure would like to get to know this creature." She smiled as she told me the story of their meeting.

"Do you know a person named Randy Wilson?" Naomi had asked Randy. She said he looked startled and wanted to know why she had mentioned that name. She reached for the little pouch that hung from her shoulder and replied, "I have a message for him."

She saw how Randy caught his breath and then laughed aloud.

"Well," he said, "how do you like that? I almost destroyed the messenger."

Naomi was puzzled. "Are you by any chance Randy Wilson?" she asked.

"Yup!" Randy said, "That's me."

Naomi quickly opened her pouch and presented the message to him. It was a legal document. She said that Randy's brown eyes turned black. Naomi could tell that he was frazzled. The papers looked legal. As it turned out, Randy told her that his wife was divorcing him. His wife had asked her to serve him the papers. It was over. Their entire marriage had been a flop.

It was obvious that Randy was upset that his wife Margaret had sent a message to the opera company on opening night of *La Boehme*. Naomi told me that she thought that his wife really knew how to hurt a guy. By just looking into his eyes, Naomi could see the determination to perform no matter what. He would not let it hurt him so badly that he would not be able to perform.

Randy suddenly realized that the little imp Naomi was still there watching him as he opened and read the note. She reached out and touched his face with her soft little hand.

"Please don't be upset," she said. "If I had known the contents of the message, I would never have delivered it just before a performance."

Romance seemed to fill the air as Naomi checked out this lovely man named Randy Wilson. He was handsome in an unusual way. He was tall, and he walked with a sexy stride. Long black hair curled around his face and framed his deep brown eyes and wonderful smile. She felt that something had made her very aware of this man.

She jumped down from the table and started out the door. Randy quickly grabbed her arm. "Please," he said, "can I see you again?"

Naomi looked at him in astonishment. "Of course," she said. I told him, "I work here as an usherette. I am here for almost every performance. See you around." With that, she scampered off to finish ushering with a broad grin on her face. She was pleased to have met such a sweet man. That was the beginning of their romance.

They had married. Three years later, they had moved to the

mountains. They loved it there. Randy was doing what he loved best. Naomi, having given birth to their first child, was drenched with love. Their little girl, Amanda, was the prize of their lives. They were in love and were very happy.

The evening was magical. The carolers sang their hearts out. Christmas carols and songs of the season reached all corners of the downstairs. The crowd that arrived to celebrate the evening drank and ate the delicious hors d'oeuvres—cheese and crackers that the staff had put out—as well as the trays of yummies, which they passed around throughout the early evening.

When the bell rang announcing dinner, they found their way to the dining room and to their assigned tables. Salads were already in place. Each table had a lovely Christmas centerpiece, which had been put together by the Flower Ladies earlier that day. Music filled the air. A fire was burning in the large quaint walk-in fireplace. Candles adorned each table, adding more to the delightful holiday feeling.

Suddenly, a wind blew into the room. It blew out the candles on some of the tables and moved toward the fireplace. The room became almost whisper quiet. Some of the guests seemed paralyzed in fear. Then just as suddenly as it began, the wind stopped.

To the amazement of those who were present, a cloud of smoke came roaring out of the fireplace, blowing ashes all over those unlucky members who had been assigned to the table nearest the fireplace. It just so happened that Naomi and Randy were sitting at that table. Everyone, who was at their table, jumped up and tried to get away from what might have been a terrible disaster.

As Naomi, Randy, and their tablemates quickly moved to the buffet room, someone said. "Look, the fire is out."

At that point, one of the guests shocked Naomi and Randy, saying in a rather surprising manner, "It's the ghost of the house letting us know that the fire was dangerous."

Randy looked quizzically at Naomi and wondered if she had been as concerned as he had been. But in her quaint way, Naomi dispelled his concerns with a broad smile and said, "A ghostly salvation?"

The lights in the ballroom blinked. The guests who had been

scurrying to leave the room suddenly stopped. As if by magic, the lights were dimmed by staff member, and then they turned on the music, playing the tender love songs of the holidays. One by one, couples got up to dance to the wonderful music. Randy captured Naomi's hand, and they took their place on the dance floor.

All seemed to again be right with the world. The Wilsons would put this evening into their memory book. Naomi kept reminding herself of how lucky she was to be part of the life in the mountains and married to the love of her life.

As the evening moved on, the staff quickly cleaned up the mess from the ashes and reset the table near the fireplace that had been targeted. Once again, the candles were lighted, and the evening was enjoyed by all who were present. Memories of this Christmas would stay in the minds of the guests, who would then pass on the story of *The Christmas of Ashes* to future members of the Stone Gate Club. It was an evening and a Christmas event that Naomi and Randy would never forget.

CHAPTER 4

LOVE IS IN THE AIR

As Howard and I arrived at the club to attend the Valentine's Day celebration, I overheard one of the member's daughters say, "I won't sleep here, Mom." Annette White had spoken these words as her mother, Genie, had gently pushed her ahead of her and onto the club's front porch. The White family had been invited to dine with old friends and to celebrate Valentine's Day.

I was told that they were looking forward to seeing the Olson family: Pepper, Peter, and their children. It had been awhile since they had been neighbors in a suburb of Chicago. Pepper told me that Annette White and Sheri Olson were close friends. They had missed each other, and they were excited to be reunited at the club for the first time since both families had moved to the mountains. The Olson family lived in nearby Pottsfield, and the Whites had opted to live in a town closer to San Regie, which was still in the mountains.

Genie had made reservations to spend the night at the club. Her daughter was dubious about staying there, as she had heard rumors that there were ghosts in older estates.

They entered the club and took off their coats. Genie, her mom, and her father, Tad, had urged Annette and her sister Merry to dress up and to wear the dressy coats, which they had been given as Christmas presents. The club had an unwritten rule: On special occasions and buffet night (each Thursday), the dress code was formal. The White family was well attired for this exciting reunion.

As they were hanging up their coats on the rack in the hallway, a warm and familiar voice said, "So how are my girls?" Peter Olson's gravelly voice reflected that not too long ago, he had been through a surgery to remove a tumor from his throat. His handsome, loving smile brought tears to their eyes. It was obvious that the girls had missed their dear friends' wonderful, loving father.

Just as Peter swept Annette into his arms for a hug, another person spoke in a sweet and lilting way. It was Pepper Olson, Peter wife, and the mother of the two Olson children, Peter Jr. (also known as Putty) and Sheri. There was more commotion behind them as the two kids moved in to get their share of the hugs. The families chatted and continued to smile and hug as they descended to the music room—another spectacular room in the Stone Gate Club.

This room was perhaps the most interesting of all the rooms. There was a unique walk-in, clay fireplace at the far end of the room. A fire was roaring in it. Tables were set with a Valentine's Day theme. On each table, there were white cloths with red overskirts, lit candles, and red and white roses for centerpieces. Sparkly red hearts hung from light fixtures around the room. The atmosphere was definitely one of love and romance.

Howard and I arrived at our table. We were seated with a group of friends we had known since our joining the club. Paula and Kent Kimball, Earl and Charlotte Spring, and a few other friends sat with to us at our table for ten. We were very aware of the table to our right because the Olsons and Whites continued to be excited over rediscovering their friendships.

Sheri and Peter (Putty) Olson and Annette and Merry occupied one side of the table. Putty decided he would sit next to Merry. During the evening, we all noticed that he paid a lot of attention to her. Occasionally, a sweet pink blush would spread over Merry's countenance.

There was much chatter and laughter throughout the room. The first course came and went. Folks at both tables were so engrossed in each other that I forgot what the salad had tasted like.

During the soup course, I looked up and saw that some of the soup had dribbled down Annette's chin. In great embarrassment, she tried to find her napkin to cover it up, but she couldn't find it.

When she had looked, it had not been in her lap or on the floor in front of her.

Noticing her frustration, Putty jumped up, as a real gentleman would, and handed her his napkin. Then he said with his deep voice, "So I bet the ghost gotcha napkin."

We watched as Annette recoiled in fear. "What did you say?" she asked. Then sputtered, "No, please don't repeat it. I'm spooked enough without a reminder of the possibility of a ghost being here." Putty threw back his head and roared with laughter. "Darn," we heard her mutter under her breath. Then we realized that the people all around us had stopped talking and that they were looking in our direction.

Annette looked all around her, was embarrassed, and said, "Sorry, but I am really frightened by ghosts."

Her mom reached over the table and patted her cheek. "My darling daughter," she said, "I want you to calm yourself." At that point, Putty interrupted and began to tell the following tale.

Please listen closely, Annette. The ghost that lives in this house is a member of a family of ghosts who were privileged to have been the servants of the original owners. I found this out while doing some research on the Stone Gate Club. They were hired by the good Doctor Eastly and his wife, who opened the house and grounds many years ago to help take care of them. No one knew who this family of servants was or where it came from. One day the family suddenly appeared at the doctor's kitchen door and asked about employment.

The doctor asked a few questions about the family members' backgrounds and the reason that they were having such a hard time. When he learned about their plight, he hired them on the spot. They became part of the club's scenery, that is, until the doctor died and the estate was sold to a group of men. The family suddenly disappeared … or so it was thought.

Putty continued with his story.

As the new male owners settled into the house, created a clubhouse, and used the grounds as a golf course and sports' area, every once in a while, someone would report strange things happening there. A bag of golf clubs went missing, only to be located on the first tee when it was time to start the game.

At the same time, newspapers went missing from the men's library, only to be replaced each day for the next guest. In the ladies' room, toilet paper went missing, but it also was replaced shortly thereafter. The same thing happened to bars of soap and wastebaskets, which had been emptied. Newspapers were retrieved from the spot on the porch where they had been delivered and were then found in their proper spot in the library. Before gatherings, ice buckets were set out by some mysterious persona.

This was all done by someone who remained a mystery, or perhaps it was a ghost. Occasionally, a figure was spotted sitting on the porch, and then it disappeared before anyone could reach it to welcome it to the club.

All of these happenings had been kept quiet when the gentlemen had decided to invite their spouses to become involved in the operation and the use of the Stone Gate Club. The female population came on board with a bang. They took over the decorating of the club. Then they insisted on having a buffet dinner one night a week. That night was called Cooks Night Out, and it became a ritual for members of the club and their families to attend.

The children looked forward to those evenings when mac and cheese was on the menu. They could play outside in warm weather and quiet games in the library when it became cooler.

On one of those cool nights in late August, the little troopers arrived to enjoy their evening to find that the checkerboard had been misplaced. They moaned and groaned to the grownups, complaining that they had nothing to do. The adults were upset because they needed the children to keep out of trouble with games to plays so that they could enjoy cocktails before dinner.

When the children were herded back to the library to try to find a game, the group was mystified. Not only was the checkerboard there but also decks of cards, a chessboard, and the chess figures. Paper and crayons had been set up for the children as well. One table had a punch bowl, cups, and napkins set out for them. There was no doubt that someone had taken the time to help the club member's children out of their dilemma, but who had done it?

A quick questioning of the staff indicated that none of them had done the deed. From that night on, everyone was on the lookout for the stranger who was helping the members of the club and accommodating their families.

As time went by, it became obvious that there were strange things happening. One night in late November, a member's family and friends were occupying bedrooms on the second floor during the weekend after Thanksgiving. After dinner, some of them decided to take walks, others wanted to rest, and the rest decided to play cards in the library.

Most of the staff had left for the night, so the club was quiet. Suddenly, there was the sound of whimpering, as if someone was crying. Agatha Lind and her husband, Barry, who were guests and friends of the Strongs (Jennifer Strong was chairman of the entertainment committee), had just come out of their bedroom. She stopped to listen and realized that the sound was coming from the linen closet next to her bedroom.

She quietly approached the door, reached for the knob, and quickly pulled the door open. Nothing was there. Then she saw the form of a young lady on the back wall of the closet. She looked around to see if there was someone behind her, whose shadow might have been projected onto the back wall of the closet. No one was there. When she looked again into the closet, she realized that the crying had stopped and the whimpering had begun again. She was appalled at what she saw. The form of the young lady had materialized. Agatha was stunned.

Before she realized what she was doing, Agatha reached for the young lady. Then she became aware that she was reaching into thin air. It had been a ghost. Agatha was too surprised to speak. Once she regained some vestige of self-control, a word or two slipped out. "Are y-y-you a g-ghost?" she asked with a trembling voice. The little figure suddenly stopped her noise, looked straight at Agatha, nodded, and then disappeared.

When I ran into the Kimball's later in the evening, they told me about the incident, which their friend Agatha Strong had relayed to them. As Agatha had descended the stairs to the first floor, she had wondered if anyone would believe her story or had heard the noises made by the strange little lady.

Her anxiety was assuaged when she realized that the folks who had been gaming in the Library were gathered in the hallway looking up toward the second floor. It was evident that they too had heard the noises. Looks of panic were all over their faces. She continued her descent, and to her amazement, they all rushed to her.

"Are you ok?" asked her husband Barry.

"Did someone hurt you?" asked another member of the group.

Agatha ran to Barry, putting her arms around his neck. "I'm okay," she said. "What you all heard was a ghost crying in the linen closet. I asked her if she was a ghost. She nodded and then disappeared. I had no idea why she was crying."

"Let's look in the closet for a clue," said another group member. So the entire entourage trooped up the stairs to look into the closet for themselves.

It became evident that the ghost had been crying because of the mess that she had found in the linen closet. Someone had gone through each shelf of sheets, towels, and linens, destroying the continuity and neatness of each item on each shelf. No wonder the ghost had been so upset. That answered our question of why there had been crying. But who was this ghost, and was it really a ghost?

Peggy Johnson, the wife of Cliff Johnson (manager of the club), got word of the incident through a staff member who was just leaving after finishing the cleanup of the kitchen. Peggy called me (Milly Murdock) at home, apologized for the lateness of the hour, and related the story as she had heard it from a staff member. I thanked Peggy, telling her that the Kimballs had already talked to me. As a member of the board of directors, I wanted to make sure that the tale was true and that everyone who was overnighting at the club was safe.

Here, Putty's story continues.

I suggested that Agatha ask the ghost questions by writing little notes to her and leaving them in very conspicuous places around the club. For the first twenty-four hours, there was no indication that the ghost had seen the notes, but by breakfast time on Sunday and to the delight of the entire group, the ghost had answered the questions.

The ghost's name was Fannie Mae Rogers. The Rogers family had settled on the land that a doctor's house had been built on. The Rogers had no money to build a house, so they put up a shanty and then went searching for odd jobs: handyman, housemaid, and laundress.

Jacob Rogers had just been fired by the railroad company that he had been working for. He had been installing new tracks for the trains to use on their trip from Boston or New York to Pottsfield. The company had furnished Jacob and his coworkers with housing in the Pottsfield area until a tragic accident occurred on the tracks just east of that city.

It was a bitter winter, and much snow and ice had built up on the tracks and at the crossings. On a very blustery morning in late January, snow flurries were drifting through the area. A two-horse carriage, which was carrying coal ash, was about to go through the crossing, which Jacob had been trying to clear the ice off.

The carriage moved forward without looking to see if the crossing gate had closed. Jacob had seen this coming, and he was hopping up and down and trying to warn the carriage driver but to no avail. As the train and the carriage entered the crossing at the same time, the train plowed into the carriage, injuring the driver and the horses. The horses had to be put down, and the carriage was a total loss. The driver sustained a head injury and a broken foot. Coal ash clogged the streets all around the tracks for weeks.

As a result of the accident, Jacob lost his job and housing for his family. He searched for days until he finally found the land where Knox now is. He put up a shanty for his family until he could find work. Not long after that, workmen began building the doctor's home on the land where Jacob had his. As the new house became larger, Jacob knew that he would have to move his family elsewhere.

He was so tired from trying to find a permanent job and a home that would keep his family protected from the bad weather that he became ill. One by one, his family members succumbed to strange diseases because of lack of a proper diet.

Once the new house was finished, his family was asked to leave the shanty. Devastated and ill, they didn't know what to do. So they approached the owners of the new house to see if they could work for them.

The doctor spoke with Jacob. He asked about Jacob's work experience. He was impressed with the story that Jacob told about the accident. Doctor Eastly was compassionate and liked what he saw in these nice people, who had been so badly treated, so he hired them on the spot. They became part of the family and worked hard to keep the property and house in good condition for the doctor and his family.

As time went by, the doctor became ill and passed away. Soon his wife and family also departed, one by one. But the Rogers' allegiance to the doctor kept working there until they also started leaving this world. However, they returned as ghosts, lived in the house, and helped the new owners acclimate as the house changed to a club.

As Putty ended the story, he realized that some of the club members from other tables around his were also listening to his story. They all clapped and started relating stories of their own encounters with the ghost family.

Annette looked over at Putty and smiled. Everyone thought that she was no longer afraid to stay overnight in one of the guest rooms on the second floor. Then she saw that the napkin, which she had earlier lost, was now draped over the back of her chair.

POKER STARS

Folks in the community of Knox seem to be surprised that anyone would think that there were ghosts at the Stone Gate Club. As there was no physical evidence of this, it was beyond their imaginations to think that any sort of mystical character could exist. So the story of ghosts at the club was simply ignored and forgotten.

One day, not too long after the story about the Christmas fireplace fire had been released, a very interesting thing occurred at the club. The poker group was meeting in the men's library. The meeting began at 6:00 p.m., and they had cocktails. Dinner service was started at 6:30 p.m. The game began as soon as they had finished dinner. After dinner, the tables were cleared, and the men took their places at the game table to begin the poker game, which would be an all-nighter. The participants were concentrating so much on the game that no one was aware of a slender figure that was hovering around the poker table.

Howard related the entire story to me later. His friend Ulysses Knowles, a treasured member of the club, had been winning. He seemed delighted when he spread out his winning hand and collected his chips. As Ulysses looked at his watch, he acted as if he might leave.

Howard thought, *He could probably get home in time to catch the 11:00 p.m. news.* As Ulysses gathered his winnings and stood up to leave, Howard noticed that he hesitated. It seemed that he had seen something—probably the figure standing next to his partner, Lee

Atwater. Suddenly, that figure moved, and all of Ulysses's chips fell on the floor.

Ulysses seemed stunned as he bent down to pick up the chips. He faltered and then must have realized that the chips were being gathered up by someone he didn't recognize. With a slight nod, he thanked the gentleman.

Once his chips were cashed in, Ulysses found his coat and umbrella and started for the door. He took one last look at the players. It seemed to dawn on him that the person who had helped him pick up the chips was nowhere in sight. Howard then saw that Ulysses was a bit overwhelmed by what had just happened to him. Ulysses returned to the table and kept joking. He was obviously looking for the person who had helped him.

Then he went to the men's room. Ulysses found that the room was empty. When he checked the other downstairs' rooms, he found no trace of the fellow. Now he was truly curious.

He returned to the library, where the poker game was still in progress. The game was going strong. Peter Olson looked up as Ulysses approached the table. Hiding his hand, Peter asked him why he had his coat on.

Laughing, Ulysses told him that he had been headed out the door when he had suddenly realized that a ghost might have been in the room. He described the man that he had seen.

Peter looked a bit puzzled and said, "I haven't seen anyone like that this evening."

Ulysses interrupted the game and asked all who were present if anyone had seen the stranger. There was a quick consensus: No one had seen a person of that description.

Now Ulysses seemed sure that he had seen a ghost. That information seemed to stun him. Howard saw Ulysses stagger around the room as he tried to get his thoughts back in order. Finally, he sat down on one of the comfortable red leather chairs. He seemed to be very confused as he sat there and to reflect on the actions taking place at the poker table. Then he stood up to leave.

Later, he said that he was sure the figure was a man's and that he had not seen him in the room before. He could not find him in any of the rooms on the first floor. It suddenly seemed to dawn on Ulysses that the man might have been a guest at the club and that he had gone up to one of the bedrooms on the second floor.

With that, he had stood up, had glanced at his watch, and had realized that it was nearly midnight. Howard saw that Ulysses was surprised at the lateness of the hour. Ulysses said that he had missed his chance to watch the late news but that he could watch one of the late shows to help him get to sleep. Since his lovely Margot had passed away, Ulysses claimed that he had difficulty relaxing and falling asleep. Once again, he proceeded to the door to leave for the night.

Later, he told Howard that just as he left the poker table, a funny, foggy feeling came over him. He stopped at Lee Atwater's side and told him that he would watch a few more minutes of Lee taking all the chips. As he sat down again, the feeling became even more pronounced. He told Howard that he must have had too much from the wine barrel.

After the next hand was played, Ulysses looked at Howard and said that he had suddenly remembered that he was a little concerned about a figure he had perhaps seen a few moments earlier. He asked Howard to check with the staff and to find out if an overnight guest might have walked in on the poker game. Ulysses seemed a bit tipsy as he told Howard that he could not pull up any image of what the person had looked like. The subject was dropped for the moment.

His friend Lee took all the chips, and as he was gloating over his winnings, the rest of the group's players were getting a bit edgy and were ready to put on their coats and leave. Lee realized that Ulysses was still there and said, "Wow! It's a bit late for you, my friend. Are you okay? You look like you might have seen a ghost."

Well, that seemed to trigger an astonished look from Ulysses. It was all that he needed to say, "Are you kidding me? I think I did see a ghost right here in this room, tonight."

"Aw, come on Ully," Lee said, calling him by his nickname, which Ulysses hated, "don't be silly. Those stories about ghosts being in this house are only on account of this house being so big and old. Why, it is considered one of the first cottages to have been built on this street. Probably one of the first that was built in this town."

"I don't need a history lesson," Ulysses said and then sighed. "I wonder if any of the staff is still in the kitchen, Howard. I know it is late, but they must have to lock up after a party. What do you think if I ask them about guests staying here tonight?"

Howard had thought that was a good way to go. So with a nod of approval from Howard, Ulysses headed for the kitchen.

When he returned, he told Howard that he had entered through the swinging door marked "employees only." Then Ulysses saw that the light was on and that there was some movement at the back of the kitchen. He was pleased and hoped to get an answer to the questions that ran through his head. But there didn't seem to be anyone in the kitchen. The door to the tavern room was propped open, and the light was still on. Because he knew that it was Saturday and a la carte night at the club, he thought that the staff was still cleaning up the room.

He looked in through the tavern room's doorway, and to his surprise, the only person he saw was Mary Ann, the sous chef. He called her name so as not to frighten her. She looked up with a start from where she was standing in front of the fireplace. She had just come into the room to make sure the fire was out, and it was.

"Why Mr. Knowles, what are you doing here at this hour?" Mary Ann gasped. Then she asked, "Can I help you?"

Grinning, Ulysses said, "I am in search of a ghost."

Mary Ann was startled. "A ghost?" she asked. She seemed obviously shaken by his answer.

"Yes, Mary Ann," replied Ulysses. "Do you know if there are guests in the upstairs' bedrooms tonight?"

"To be honest, I am not sure," she replied. "Mr. Johnson, our managing chef, didn't tell me. But that doesn't mean there aren't any. I tell you what, if you want to check, we can go upstairs and try the doors to the rooms. If they are unlocked and open, there is no guest in the room."

Leading the way up the stairs, Mary Ann tried the door to the first room on the left in the upper hallway (the Knox Room), only to find it locked. They wondered what that meant. Were there any guests in the room?

Ulysses and Mary Ann continued to try the doors on the second floor but found that they were all locked. They were about to give up and return to the first floor. As they started to descend the stairs, a little hiss came from the bathroom in the hallway behind them.

Later, Mary Ann said that she had jumped at the sound as she had felt a ripple of fear. Ulysses claimed that he had also been a bit nervous, as he hadn't been sure of what he had heard. They both wondered aloud if the bathroom had a radiator. If it did, was it truly steaming and hissing? Was it the bathroom radiator, or could it be the ghost trying to let them know that it did exist?

Ulysses told me the entire story when we were at the Thursday-night buffet together. He asked me to try to find out if the bathroom pipes were really steaming and hissing, as I was at the time, a member of the house committee and on the board of governors for the club.

A few days later, I was in the club for a meeting. I made sure to get the item regarding the hissing we had heard on the manager Cliff's *to-do* list.

Sometime later, Cliff called me at home and asked who had requested the checking of the hissing and steaming bathroom. When I told him, he didn't speak for a second and then laughed and said, "I thought it might be Ulysses."

I asked, "Why are you laughing?"

Cliff replied, "I don't think Ulysses is having a wonderful life right now. His lovely wife recently passed away, and he seems to be quite lost for something to do that will capture his mind and imagination. So I am not going to think this might be a ghost." With that, he hung up, leaving me to ponder about the entire event.

This was one more indication of what might really be happening at the Stone Gate. It seemed obvious to me that whatever had caused the incident to roll around in the mind of my friend Ulysses was all to the good. It seemed to help reawaken his life. Now he had something to think about instead of loneliness and the way his life had changed since his loving wife, Margot, had died.

Soon it became evident that Ulysses was getting hold of his life once again. He volunteered to help with programs at the club, and he was seen in the company of Tammy Green, Charlotte Spring's aunt.

HAPPY BIRTHDAY

On a very pleasant day in April, I drove Annette and Merry White and their mom, Genie, to the Stone Gate Club. As we approached the stone pillars that lead to the club's driveway, many memories cropped up in my imagination. I wondered if Annette had a queasy feeling that something was going to happen today, just like the last time they had been at the club.

She later admitted that she was focused on strange things happening around her and was tuned into her feeling of mysticism. "Milly, remember the napkin episode?" she asked me, referring to her first visit to the Stone Gate Club.

As my car reached the club, someone was sitting on a porch bench, which faced the croquet court. I parked the car in the empty parking lot. The gals got out and walked up to the porch. It was empty. I knew it was, or at least I thought it was. That ghost was doing it again. It was messing with my mind.

I must find out more about this ghost. If Annette and I are afraid of a ghost, imagine how a little child might feel, I thought as I imagined a family with young children who might be spooked by such antics arriving.

As we were entering the club, we heard another car arriving. It was our new friend Holly Grant, who had asked us all to attend a luncheon in honor of Pepper Olson's birthday. The Whites and Olsons had been good friends for a long time. It was also noted that Merry White and Putty Olson, the two older children, had a little *thing* going. They couldn't take their eyes off each other when they were together.

Annette and Mary told me that as they waited for me to park my car, they had been standing in the hallway. As Annette made a quick turn toward the men's library, she thought she saw the bottom of a skirt swish by. She ran into the room and said in a loud voice, "I know you are here. Do something to let me know it's true."

Merry poked her head into the library and with a sly smile, asked Annette to whom she had been talking. Annette shrugged her shoulders and with a quick look around the room, left to rejoin the others in the hallway.

Our group had expanded to include other guests. Walking into the Tavern Room, we were all very aware of the festive atmosphere of a birthday party. Balloons were hanging from the ceiling. Crepe paper was strung from corner to corner. Tables were set with soft pink tablecloths and darker pink napkins. The centerpieces had lovely pink, red, and purple roses with white baby's breath, which were in silver vases. A corner table was piled high with packages, which had been wrapped in colorful paper. The whole effect was magical.

The excited chatter grew louder, until someone used their table utensils to make the noise of a chime. It worked to quiet down the lively conversations.

"Please, ladies, find your seats," said Holly Grant, who was the hostess of the party. "The place cards will tell you where you are to sit. Before we are served our luncheon, I would like to take a moment to say a few words."

Holly stood near the bar as she addressed the group. Because she had been a member of the club for quite some time, she had become the party-giver and coordinator of events. Those who held special parties and events throughout the year always consulted Holly. In addition to her party and decorating talents, she was a very clever and well-known artist. That talent showed in all the things she attempted to accomplish.

She continued, "As you all know, Pepper Olson is a relatively new member of the Stone Gate Club. I am pretty sure that she enjoys the club as much as do all the members. However, she has had some hesitation because of the stories of ghosts residing here."

Once she mentioned ghosts, the entire room quieted down, as if in a stupor. I was also amazed as she continued, saying, "I am here to tell you that the stories you have been hearing about this lovely club are simply not true."

The sound of a glass being broken shocked the entire room. Peggy, the club's hostess, was standing behind the bar, and she looked puzzled. She shrugged her shoulders and looked as if she was unsure of where the noise had come from. No one could figure it out.

Holly continued as if speaking to a ghost. "We don't need that extra noise, please. So if you are here, just sit down quietly while we enjoy our afternoon and the party."

The ladies seemed to relax as Holly began again to recount her story. "Please know that even if there were ghosts, they would be the friendliest in town. It is well known that many of the old estates and some of the loveliest current venues open to the public boast of ghosts. I happen to have had an encounter at one of these lovely venues a summer ago. It is still vivid in my mind, but it can also be explained. I cannot be convinced that it was truly a ghost."

Holly began telling her story of what had happened a year ago at Charing Hall. Here is her tale.

I entered the front door of Charing Hall. There was a docent sitting at a registration desk to my right as I walked in. She was ready with her little speech about the events taking place at the restoration. One of them was a display of beautiful cloth dolls representing the early days in the mountains. I also make dolls, so I was very interested in seeing what the competition was displaying.

After escorting me into the rooms where the dolls were located, the docent left me and returned to her desk. I walked around the room, admiring the beautifully dressed vintage dolls. They were vastly different from the ones I make, so I was not too jealous of them.

As I became absorbed in their display, I was unaware of anyone else in the room. I heard a little noise coming from a corner off to my left. It sounded like someone was scraping the floor. I was curious, so I walked over to where the sound had come from. Nothing was there. Then I heard the sound behind me.

I quickly turned my head, and I was astonished to see a doll's head turn, or so I thought it did. I headed in her direction, only to be spooked by the sound, which now came from the first place I had looked. The doll that was there seemed to look the same way as it had earlier, but I was not sure. Its head looked the same, but was it?

In great excitement, I returned to the registration desk. The staff had changed, and now, a gentleman was sitting behind the desk. His name tag said that he was Milton Farber. I asked him if I could speak to the lady docent who had been there earlier. He looked at me with astonishment. "Who was it that you saw?" he asked.

I was puzzled. "How long have you been here at this desk?"

"I've been here for about an hour," Milton replied.

I looked at my watch. Had I been wandering around the doll display for over an hour? I asked him the name of the person whom he had replaced.

"Why it was Tom Norman. That is our usual staff here on Mondays."

I really wanted to get to the bottom of this. "No, no," I retorted. "I mean the lady who was here."

"Lady?" Milton quizzed. With that he said, "There are no ladies here on Monday. Please understand, Miss, we are entirely a volunteer staff. We try very hard to make sure our guests are escorted and are given a clear description of the venue. I personally have been a volunteer here for over four years. I very much enjoy meeting the guests and being a docent. I know everyone on the schedule. No lady is scheduled to work with me on Mondays, nor has there been during the four years I have volunteered here."

"Okay," I said. "So who was the person that escorted me to see the doll exhibit?"

Milton asked, "What did she look like?"

"I don't recall what the person looked like. I only remember her garb: a straight navy-blue skirt with a stiff-collared white shirt. Her hair was done up in a bun. I think it may have crossed my mind that she was in costume."

With that, he put his hands behind his head, looked at me with a funny grin, and said, "Oh, are you lucky. You have met the ghost of Charing Hall."

That was the tale of my visit to Charing Hall and a possible ghost sighting. By this time, I saw that the group of ladies had begun to relax. Some of them were even relating stories of some of the strange happenings that they had encountered while attending events at that local attraction.

Then I noticed that another member had stood up, and she wanted to tell of the time she lost one of her earrings in the ladies' room at The Fount. Mabs Henry, the wife of our local fire commissioner and a longtime member of the club, said that she was very upset, as the jewelry had been passed down to her from her mother and that she treasured it. To lose one of the set was simply unthinkable.

She said that as she was leaving, she became aware of a lovely young woman following her. The girl tapped her shoulder and held out her hand. There was the earring. Mabs was so grateful that she started to tear up. Then the girl vanished. Mabs wondered where she had gone.

Mabs went back to the front desk and asked to have the young woman located. The staff simply looked at her in amazement and then told her that there was no such person on the staff. Mabs looked in my direction and said, "Milly, why don't you tell the story of the garage-door opener?"

So I launched into my story. I parked my car next to the entrance of the Stone Gate Club's porch. When I returned to my car after having attended a meeting of the board of governors, I realized that the garage-door opener, which had been attached to the sun visor, was no longer there. I was just furious with myself that I had been so careless and had evidently lost the opener. Luckily, we had an extra.

The next week, I had to attend a finance-committee meeting at the club. A snowstorm had covered the grounds with about four inches of the white stuff. The driveway to the club had been plowed.

I parked in the same spot that I had parked in the week before. I had a funny feeling as I looked at the snow piled up in front of the parking spaces. As I got out of the car and looked at the piles of snow, I saw what I thought was the opener … and it was. Now how do you explain that?

The party continued. Lunch was served. Penny opened some of her gifts. Time seemed to fly by. One by one, the guests left, all aglow from the lovely party. Genie, Merry, Annette, and I were among the last to wend our way to the front hallway.

Merry nudged Annette and said in a joking manner, "I wonder if you got a response from the ghost you thought you saw when we arrived."

Chuckling as if to herself, Annette said, "Well, there is one way to find out."

Entering the library, she said in a quiet voice, "Hello, my mysterious friend. Can you let me know that you are still here?"

We had followed her into the library. We could see the amazement on Annette's face as the drapes at the window started to rustle. There was movement and a sound like someone trying to sing. We all were struck dumb. Annette moved toward the window and said in a very low voice, "Thank you. I shall treasure this day." The drapery swayed once more.

Merry, Genie, and I stood inside the doorway to the library watching the events that were taking place with Annette. We were breathless. No longer would we doubt the stories about ghosts at the Stone Gate Club.

CHAPTER 7

SMOKY HALLOWEEN

Time rolled on, and some of the incidents were shuffled under the carpet. Howard and I talked about the ghostly implications while at home over dinner. We concluded that there was no immediate danger to any of the club members, but no matter what, we could not escape the ghostly feeling that someone or something was present at the Stone Gate Club

The executive committee of the board of governors gathered late one afternoon in the men's Library for a meeting. They pooh-poohed the entire idea of a ghost being present. I asked if I could read a short story about the ghost, which a member of the club had written. Afterward, the board members were clearly not impressed with the story. They let me know their feelings by yawning and looking bored. When the meeting was about to end, a puff of smoke suddenly came from the recently cleaned and long-ago closed fireplace.

"Okay, you guys, explain that!" I said. They had nothing to say.

Speaking of the club's board of governors, they usually met at a set time in the men's library. This room was handsome. The walls were lined with bookcases, which were backed with a baize deep-green fabric. Pictures of hunting scenes and former members of the club adorned the walls over the bookcases. Memorabilia was on display in glassed-in display cases. These are examples of how deeply the members wanted to preserve the history of their dear old club.

Now let's get back to the board members. They were a special group of people. Their interest in the club was their main goal. On a monthly basis, the main thrust of those who met in the men's library was to help keep the club alive, active, and financially stable and the members happy. Those who met each month gave no credence to ghosts until it became evident that things were happening that could not be explained, such as smoke coming from a closed fireplace, this time, in one of the upstairs bedrooms. In bedroom number two, the fireplace had not been operational since 1925. The damper was closed, and there was no evidence that the fireplace had been in use. So how could smoke be coming into the bedroom?

As a representative of the board, I spoke with Shawna and Elliott Crow, the guests occupying the room in question. They seemed to be shocked and scared. They said that they had called the manager, Cliff Johnson, and had related the story to him three hours earlier. They wanted to move to another room.

They told me that Cliff had just laughed and had asked them not to worry. He had reminded them that it was Halloween weekend. He had said that the entertainment committee had been working hard to make sure the guests were part of the upcoming celebration. He had also said that the Crows should not be afraid of the smoke because the fireplace was closed. The smoke had come from a can, which someone had put in the fireplace, to help guests enjoy the Halloween holiday at the club. The Crows were convinced that the smoke was an omen of things to come, and they were correct.

As the weekend moved on, Howard and I watched the guests as they congregated in the buffet room. The club had provided a plan that suggested what the guests could do for entertainment during the daylight hours at the club. We offered to provide transportation to the many venues in and around Knox.

The guests were invited to visit the Charing Hall restoration, which was nearby and a wonderful tour of an older home. It was known as for its cottages, which were restored to reflect the early nineteenth-century era. Then there was the Dorman Mockwell Museum. Many guests toured that auspicious venue. On their way back to the club, they often visited the acclaimed Mountains Flaming Gardens. It just so happened that the Harvest Festival at the Gardens was taking place. There was much to see, do, and … buy.

After traveling all around the area, many of the guests opted to return to the club and relax. They showered and changed in readiness for the evening's events, napped, or put their feet up and read books by their favorite authors.

At 6:00 p.m., the bar on the porch opened. Halloween decorations were throughout the first floor. The porch had torchlights at every corner. There were bales of hay upon which sat people dressed as scary characters for the event. Some were even dressed as ghosts.

Pumpkins and cornstalks were attached to the lampposts at the main door to the club. Bats hung all around the porch, suspended by invisible cord from the ceiling. There was even a cauldron just past the far end of the porch on the lawn. Witches were tending the fire under the pot, from which arose fragrant steam. Little did the guests know that the steam was cooking mussels and clams. These would soon be on trays together with dipping sauce and would be served by the witches to those who desired them.

As Howard and I arrived, we heard much laughter and conversation on the porch. We were excited to see that most of the members were attired in Halloween costumes. Here was Mistress Mary with her little (stuffed) lamb, enjoying her glass of white wine. Then there was the evil monster with a broken arm, sipping his martini held in his good hand. He looked evil, wore a very ugly mask, had blood coming out of him, and had his swollen leg on top of the table in front of him. He complained that his wife had been angry with him for giving away some of her favorite candy to the little ones who had come trick-or-treating. So she had cut off his leg.

Off in a corner, little Miss Muffet sat. She was balancing her manhattan as she sat on her tuffet. A roar of laughter went up when she decided to jump up as a little old spider tried to sit down beside her. The manhattan went up into the air and came back down on the spider, soaking his costume to the enjoyment of the crowd. It couldn't have happened to a better candidate. Sonny Brackett was not admired by some of the members. The club members had a soft spot for Sonny's wife, Sheila. She was playing Miss Muffet this Halloween. All those who knew her were astounded that she had a husband like

Sonny. He was obliviously rude to her and at times, was vocally abusive. Most of the group on the porch felt sorry for her.

There was a lull in the conversations, and the dinner bell rang. Hungry guests, who had been nibbling on cheese and crackers and delicious shellfish and dip, rushed for the door to the dining room. They found their tables and sat down to enjoy the yummy salad, which was already at each place setting.

A ghostly light glowed from the majestic clay fireplace at the end of the room. As the evening progressed, the light seemed to shine brighter and brighter. It began as a white light but changed color. Guests who had been surprised at seeing something similar in their bedrooms earlier that evening were not concerned. However, members who had come for an evening of merriment and the celebration of All Hallows' Eve were a bit of concerned.

The light traveled throughout the room until it came to rest on one table in particular—the table where Miss Muffet sat with her dinner partners. The light was now green. Most of the attendees realized that the light was probably part of the planned events. However, the fact was disputed by Ruthy Alcott, who was in charge of the evening's decorations and happenings. Ruthy was just as surprised as the others were. She wondered where the light was coming from too. At the last moment, had Jennifer decided to pull a fast one and fool even Ruthy?

That year, Ruthy was a member of the decorating committee. She and her husband, Hank, had been long-standing members of the club and had helped to make events like Halloween and Valentine's Day memorable occasions. Now that Hank had passed away, Ruthy was always available to lend a hand.

Jennifer Strong, chair of the entertainment committee, was a real find. She had great ideas for events, as well as being willing to help with any of the decorations for each event. Jennifer had been a member for a long time. She and her husband, Bert, were always willing to help with whatever the club needed. She and Bert also wanted to find out what was behind the strange light. Bert had been one of the members who worked on the decorations. He had helped decorate the music room.

As the staff cleared away the salad plates and brought out the clam chowder for the soup course, a strange thing happened. The folding table that was stacked with empty salad plates near Miss Muffet's table collapsed. Then the one at the next serving station did the same thing. As the third one started to give up its dishes, Rory the waiter grabbed it before it also fell. "What a mess!" yelled one of the members.

Suddenly and one after another, the tray tables were standing up again while the dishes remained in a heap on the floor. Staff members were visibly upset. They couldn't believe that all those dishes had been dumped on the floor. Before they could dwell on the why question, they needed to keep moving and clean up the broken china.

Most of the dishes weren't broken. It was as if someone had played another trick on that Halloween evening and had tried to capture the attention of all those who were present. It worked.

Meanwhile, Lila, the bartender, was just coming down the stairs with a wine bottle in each hand. She was intending to refill the glasses of those folks who wanted it. She was just in time to watch some of the falling plates. While doing so, she dropped a couple of the wine bottles, tripped, and fell right onto the lap of Jonathan Cargrove, who was the president of the local Bank of New England and a prominent member of the Stone Gate Club. He was just as surprised as Lila was. He blustered and tried to help her stand up. Lila's name tag caught in Jonathan's mustache. He howled in pain when she tried to get up from his lap.

Jonathan's wife, Jean, went into active mode. She wanted to pull Lila up onto her feet and get her back into service. As Jean stood up and tried to take a step toward Lila, she slipped on a piece of lettuce from a salad plate, which had fallen off the tray table. As she slipped, she took the tablecloth with her, scattering the remaining items that were still on the table all over the floor.

Meanwhile, the wine bottles Lila had been carrying were rolling across the floor toward the fireplace. They hit the corner of the clay fireplace and exploded. Folks at nearby tables were showered with fragments of glass and splashes of wine.

The whole scene was howling funny, and that is just what the guests in the room did: howl. Once the laughter died down, staff members realized that things were out of control. They began sweeping up the damage, helping those with glass shards in their hair and laps, picking the pieces up without cutting themselves, and resetting the Cargrove's table. Then they tried to serve the chowder without dropping it. The staff was as shaken as the members were.

Lila suggested and the club president concurred that members be offered a free refill of their favorite beverage. To some extent, that helped ease the tension, but questions still floated around the room about the light, the incidents on the porch, and now the tray tables. What was at work here? Surely, the entertainment committee hadn't planned all these extraordinary events.

By the time all the mess had been cleared away, guests had been summoned to the buffet table. They filled their plates with sumptuous helpings of the chef's best. The room was unusually quiet, and conversations were low-keyed.

Many of the guests debated about what had caused the ruckus. Most of them remained baffled about the reason. Some of them suggested that the ghost might be involved. But then they wondered why a ghost would go to such lengths to make these things take place, especially on Halloween.

The dessert table was again filled with yummy pies, cakes, and ice cream. They would help the guests finish off the greatest fun-filled Halloween event that anyone could remember at the Stone Gate Club. But there were still questions.

During the next weekend of events, several crazy things happened at the club. On movie night during a wonderful film about a dog, the screen went blank. Morris Lord, the member in charge of the showing, got up to see what was wrong. As he crossed the room headed for the TV, the movie came back on. After that, it happened at least two more times. The folks who were in charge could not explain why the movie kept blanking out. Was it the ghost of the Stone Gate Club trying to make sure that people knew the ghost did indeed exist?

CHAPTER 8

NEW BOARD OF GOVERNORS

On a balmy day late in May, members of the Stone Gate Club gathered for their annual meeting. President Harlow (Harey) Thornton called the meeting to order at the appointed hour. The meeting was held in the music room. There were important issues to be voted on by the members as well as voting new members into office for the board of directors.

As a member of the board, I felt that I had to attend the annual meeting. Howard and I had just arrived in time to hear Harey call the meeting to order. We had been waylaid by our new pet: a sweet little rescue puppy of mixed breeds. She had decided that she was going with us no matter where we went. Her name was Angelique or Angel for short. How we loved her. So of course, we couldn't just leave her alone. We had go to the pet store and buy a new pet carrier for the car so that she could wait for us in the car and not sit alone at home while we attended the meeting at the club. The trip to the pet store made us late for the meeting.

Following the procedures, which had been outlined in the meeting's agenda, and after reading the minutes of the prior year's meeting, the annual meeting got underway. A vote was called for, and the minutes were approved. Harey continued down the list of items on the agenda. Once the agenda was completed, the most important issue was presented. It had become a contentious issue among club members.

The board had tried numerous times to make the issues very clear for us. They had tried to help clear up any confusion as to what our roles as club members would be, concerning the sale of club-owned land. Finally, a group of investors had presented a proposal that had been approved. The board had voted on it and then had presented it to the membership at large.

The annual meeting was the time when all of the issues surrounding the sale of this portion of land would be unveiled. There was much contentious discussion during the meeting, but it became clear that most of the members were in favor of the sale.

Harey asked for a vote to accept the sale of the land. The vote was taken, and the members who were present accepted it. The proxy votes were counted, and the total was in favor of the sale. Board members then retired to the library to nominate and to vote on the officers for the coming year.

I sensed that something wasn't quite right. After doing a head count of those who were present, the outgoing president, Harey Thornton, observed that there were sixteen members present. There should only have been fifteen. I asked for a roll call. Harey was shocked by my insistence, but he complied.

I noticed that he was quietly scanning the faces of those in the room. He started when he looked at a pretty face, which was across the table from me. I could see the questions on his face: Now where did that pretty face come from, and what was her name? Was she a person who had just appeared, hoping to listen in on the meeting? Perhaps she was even a reporter from the *Mountain Times*, who wanted front-page news of the past hour's events. After all, the selling of the land was a big topic in the mountains. It had already impacted the entire club, as well as those folks who abutted the club land.

Harey slowly walked around the large table that had been set up for the meeting. June Devers was speaking about how wonderful it was to be appointed to the board and what a lovely club she had joined. Just as Harey reached June to acknowledge her comments, he noticed an empty chair to the right of Larry Gross. That was where the pretty-faced woman had been sitting. As he looked around the room, there was no sign of her. Harey seemed to be a bit perplexed. He later told me that he thought she might be the ghost of the Stone

Gate Club. If not, had the ghost been present in another form, that is, if there truly was a ghost at the Stone Gate Club? Smiling, Harey turned to June and thanked her for her comments.

With that, Harey excused himself and withdrew to the bar room. As the Annual meeting was usually held on Thursday night just before the scheduled buffet, the bulk of those attending the annual meeting were staying to enjoy the dinner.

The bar was open. Howard and I talked with folks about the land sale and other items of interest around the town of Knox. We were standing at the bar awaiting our libations. Harey approached the bar to order his martini. As I watched him, I noticed that he look surprised. I then realized that the pretty woman was standing in the corner watching the crowd.

Harey gave his drink order and then started toward the corner of the room, which was just beyond the bar. I realized that he had spotted Pretty Face. His look became one of disappointment when he determined that she had eluded him again.

I wondered where she was now and what had intrigued Harey about this lovely looking woman. She was obviously attractive. She had large eyes that were deep green, a tall striking figure, and long dark hair. She seemed to be well dressed. My guess was that Harey was very taken with her and that he wanted to know whom she was and what she was doing at the Stone Gate Club.

As we stood in the bar room enjoying our cocktails, we heard the door to the library open. The new officers came out and headed for their drinks at the bar. The members congratulated the new officers and greeted them. The new president, Larry Gross, was accompanied by his charming wife, Carole. The treasurer and secretary, along with their wives, were also present at the bar.

Harey fought his way through the crowd at the bar to Larry and started to congratulate him when he spotted her again. This time, she was back in the library, and she seemed to be engrossed in reading something. I wondered how she had escaped into the library without us seeing her leave the bar.

I was intrigued by Harey's antics. I saw him look into the library.

I watched as his expressions changed. Instead of moving into the room and trying to talk to her, he waited just outside on the steps to the second floor. It was pure luck that he did. When he looked again, she had disappeared once more. He said later that he assumed that we would have seen anyone leaving the library and that she had not left the room ... or had she?

Larry, the new president of the board, had been startled by Harey suddenly walking away from their conversation at the bar. I observed Larry as he watched Harey move into the hallway, stand in front of the library's door, and watch something that was going on in that auspicious room. He must have been as interested in Harey's antics as I was. But by then, Larry was approached by another member, and I think he probably tabled his thoughts about Harey.

I saw that Harey was hailed by his wife, Ann. It was time to think about eating dinner. I watched as she quizzed him. She asked where he had been and why it had taken him so long. I listened all of Ann's questions.

But Harey, probably in an effort to keep from frightening Ann, was mute. Of course, that didn't sit too well with his wife. I would guess that Harey thought to himself, *Oh well. I'll hear about this in the car and probably all the way home to Grande Harrington.*

At dinner, Larry Gross, the new president, made some announcements, introduced the new officers of the board, and asked for a thank-you round of applause for the outgoing officers and board members. Upcoming events were announced, and members were urged to attend and participate as often as they were able.

The events committee had some interesting items on their calendar. I had my phone with me, so I recorded the upcoming events with an eye on discussing our attendance of them with Howard. The next round-table evening was being advertised as one of the best of the year. The directors of the Mountain City Museum, Mountains Flaming Gardens, The Fount, Shakespeare and Friends, Dorman Mockwell, and Charing Hall were all invited to attend this round-table event.

Later, I learned from Larry that reservations were coming in fast and furiously for this major event. Even folks from other clubs and from around the area wanted come and view the excitement of the upcoming event.

I said to Howard, "Imagine being able to learn about the events at The Fount, the Mountains Flaming Gardens, the Charing Hall restoration, and others, without having to plan a visit to each one individually."

More reservations began to flow into the system like magic. I kept in touch with the staff of the club to make sure that they could accommodate all the folks who were anxious to attend such a wonderful event.

Without a doubt, the music room, which had been set up auditorium style, could handle well over one hundred seats. But adding a dinner was really going to be an issue. Where would they put one-hundred folks for dinner and still have the space for all of them to have cocktails prior to eating. Cliff Johnson, the wonderful chef and manager of the club, decided to investigate setting up a large tent on the croquet court just off the porch.

It was early spring, and there was no telling what the weather would be like. So it was a factor. However, not to take a chance would be foolish. The people wanted a wonderful event. Cliff would provide it.

CHAPTER 9

THE ROUND TABLE EVENT

A small group usually attended round-table night, so it was usually held in the music room of the club. However, this time due to the large number of reservations, it was done in a different manner. Dinner was being served in a large tent on the lawn and was next to the croquet court. The bars were on the porch and inside in the bar room.

The music room was set up as if it was an auditorium. Tables with displays were against the walls and gave information about the different venues being represented by their directors and staffs. Large posters and flyers were available in the buffet room, just a few steps above the music room. Aids for each venue were there to answer the questions of those who were attending the round-table event.

Parking was at a premium for this special night, but Howard and I and Harey and Ann found spots adjacent to each other along the driveway that led to the club. We strolled down the driveway to the club's porch, where we met other members who were excited to be included in the evening's special event. More than that was in the air. I felt that people were also uncertain and that something like a little magic was there.

Because the weather was warmer than we had originally thought it might be, we realized that the bar on the porch was the busiest one. Howard and I saw that the guests of honor were all assembled on one side of the porch and were being hounded by members and guests, who had questions about each of their special venues. We recognized reporters from the local newspapers hovering there as well, hoping to get some pictures and news for their late editions.

Howard, Harey, Ann, and I joined the group but as I found out later, not before Harey spotted that pretty face once again. He had told himself, *Harey, this is quite impossible.* She had sat there in one of the wicker chairs and had watched the crowd.

Shirley Champion, a long-standing member of the club, moved as if she was going to sit in that chair. As she did, PF (Pretty Face), as Harey was now calling her, stuck out her foot and tripped Shirley so that she landed facedown on the porch's floor. Her drink went flying into the air and spilled all over Janet Hudson and her guest, Tony Rydell. I arrived on the scene just after the event happened. I was nonplussed at the picture that presented itself to the guests.

Later, Harey told me that he couldn't help but laugh because the scene was so absurd. Of course, the chair was empty. PF was gone again.

Meanwhile, poor Shirley was attended to by her husband, John, and a number of her friends. In falling, she had scraped her nose, and it was bleeding profusely down the front of her lovely cream-colored linen pantsuit.

I followed her as she was ushered into the ladies' room for some first aid. We found the first-aid kit, and a few moments later, she emerged with a wide bandage across her nose and a swollen area around her left eye. She held cold compresses in place and claimed that she was fine. She only wanted to have a drink and stay for the upcoming evening's event. We thought she was a very good sport.

However, Janet Hudson was not a happy camper. Her outfit for the evening, which was a lovely silk shirt and white pants, was drenched with booze. Her friend and guest for the evening, Tony Rydell, had also been showered by alcohol. It didn't show up on his sport coat as vividly as it did on Janet's clothing. While trying to clean up the mess and having difficulty with the stains, Janet stomped off the porch and into the ladies' room.

By this time, Shirley had left. It was a good thing that she had, as we all knew that Janet was about to give her a piece of her mind. We helped Janet clean up her shirt and pants and said that we hoped they looked okay for the rest of the evening. She didn't want to leave until the round-table event had happened. So she thanked us and left to go find Tony.

The bell rang, announcing the beginning of the dinner hour. We all grabbed our cocktails, went into the music room to find our seats for later in the evening, and then found our tables in the tent for that evening's dinner. We sat down to enjoy the fresh shrimp salad that was placed before us. Then we ate the soup of the day, which was a delicious French-onion soup that our favorite sous chef, Janice O'Brien, had concocted. I always wanted her to publish a soup cookbook but to no avail. Janice was too busy trying to manage her job and working to help her family and elderly parents. She didn't need an extra job writing a book.

The tent was abuzz with conversations. Janet Hudson and Tony Rydell were at our table, along with the outgoing president of the board, Harey Thornton, and his wife, Ann. Things were a bit stiff during the first course. Once the soup was served and the salad plates were removed, everyone's stiffness seemed to relax.

Janet and Tony began a conversation about the wonderful clay fireplace enclosure in the music room. We all had tales to add to the conversation. Some of the talk was about a ghost perhaps being at the Stone Gate. The idea was shuffled under the carpet. I concluded that this was not a topic of interest for most of the members. Yet it still had a stranglehold on my imagination.

The history of the fireplace was something that most of the club members didn't know about. It was intriguing when anyone began to talk about the origins of the clay and what the figures surrounding the opening to the fireplace represented. Were they a Native American design or an image that had developed in the imagination of the original owner and builder, Dr. Eastly? I fear that this question has never been answered.

As the evening continued, Harey and Ann excused themselves and went to find their seats for the round-table event in the music room. Harey kept watch over the fireplace. It seemed to float in front of his eyes. *No, no,* he told himself, as he later explained to Howard and me. Yet as he watched the fireplace, it seemed to glow with a light from behind it.

Then he saw her again. PF was sitting on one of the clay seats inside the fireplace. She was adorned in the loveliest gown that he had ever seen (He jokingly told me, "You and Ann could take a lesson from PF on how to dress up"). He thought she was smiling at him until suddenly, there was no one there.

Ann, Janet, and I were sitting near each other. We had begun speculating on the fire in the fireplace and wondering why it had been there on such a warm evening. Ann suggested that one of the ladies had become chilled and had asked someone to start a fire. I reflected on a theory that had been rattling around in my head during the dinner hour. What if it had something to do with the ghost?

As I turned to speak to the ladies about such a suggestion, I caught Ann looking at her husband in a quizzical way. As I turned to look at him, it seemed that Harey was in a trance. He was staring at the fireplace as if something more than a fire was there. I wondered if the woman that he was always talking about and who seemed to disappear each time he claimed to have seen her, might be involved.

Just then, the fire flared up. It was startling to see the blaze do so. It made an impression on all of those who were seated close to the fireplace. The evening was not cool enough to enjoy a fire in that noted fireplace. I asked Rory, our waiter, why there was a fire. Rory seemed to be as puzzled as we were. He had no explanation.

The program began, and it was most enjoyable. There was a presentation from the Mountain City Museum, which told of their wonderful new programs. A short story was told by the director of the Fount, which was written by Idithe Barton. Dorman Mockwell had a lovely display of artwork by local artists, some of whom were present and able to answer questions about their work.

The director of the Flaming Garden sang the praises of those members of the Stone Gate Club who were also involved in work at the gardens. He also invited anyone present to become involved in the Mountains Flaming Gardens. Then there was Shakespeare and

Friends. They arrived with a crew of actors, who gave a short but delightful rendition of one of Shakespeare's famous plays.

The evening was a total success until the lights went out. The whole club was in darkness. The staff hurriedly scampered around to find candles and flashlights to help guide the guests. A siren wailed, and then bright lights shone through the darkness as the Knox Fire Department's largest fire truck came down the driveway.

What was happening? Everyone stood transfixed. As the fire truck came to a halt in front of the porch and the fire crew scampered down to run into the club, it was frightening. Members and guests started to leave. They rushed to their cars. Some of them stumbled in the dark and forgot where their cars were. It became an awkward but funny scene.

Howard and I decided to leave also. We headed to the parking lot and ran into Harey. He was looking at something in his hand. Just then, his wife, Ann, appeared. Harey looked startled, as if he was uncertain of his next move. Then he began relating a story to us. We were so interested that we forgot about looking for our car.

When Harey reached his car, PF appeared next to the driver's door. Harey had reached the end of his patience. He grabbed for her, caught the sleeve of her lovely lace dress, and then once again, she was gone. But now he had proof. The sleeve of her dress was clenched in Harey's hand.

He wondered what he should do. Harey was in a quandary. As he watched members leave the parking lot and escape the events of the darkened Stone Gate Club and the firefighters finishing up their jobs of investigating any possible fires or hazards in or around the club, his demeanor calmed down.

Ann said that she had taken a break to head for the ladies' room when the lights had gone out. She was scared, and she began looking for Harey. She caught up with him at the car and after the incident with PF had taken place.

She said she noticed the lace that was in his fist and asked him what had happened. She said that he was hesitant to tell her because he thought it might frighten her. Then it seemed to dawn on him that

PF was not a fearful creature. He thought she was lovely to look at and that she always seemed to be in places before tragedy struck. It was almost as if she was signaling to people to be watchful and that something was not quite right. She was truly an asset to the club. She was a friendly ghost.

Ann then confessed that she had noticed that some things had not been as they should have been. When she arrived at the ladies' room on the first floor as the sirens were wailing, she opened the door to the bathroom and saw that light was coming from underneath the door to one of the stalls. Ann was a bit surprised, but then she thought that someone had done the same thing she had done: put a little flashlight into her purse. One could never tell when one might need it.

She used the bathroom. She was washing her hands when she felt a slight breeze blow though the room. Startled, she turned around and caught sight of a person leaving the room. She spoke out, "Guess you brought a flashlight too, huh?" There was no answer. There was no one there. Harey put an arm around Ann's shoulders and thanked her for sharing her story with him.

"Do you think it might have been PF? You seem very interested in this lady. Should I be a little worried?" she asked.

"Gee Ann, I really cannot answer that question, but it surely might seem so." Harey looked at her a little sheepishly. He shimmied through that suggestion from Ann by saying, "Let's just keep our eyes open the next time we are at the club. Perhaps we'll see something more concrete to explain all the little incidents of the past few weeks. I don't think we need to worry about the club, as I would guess that alleged ghosts are protecting the property and are friendly."

Harey said, "Now, my dear, I think it is time to get some needed shut-eye. How about we retire?" With that, Ann and Harey said, "Good night," to us. Howard and I had plenty to discuss once we got home from that unusual evening.

CHAPTER 10

FAMILY FUN

I consider myself a seasoned and well-trained hostess because I am a wife and mother. However, a time comes when I must put aside my pride and admit that a house full of relatives is fine for a night or meal. After that, the work that goes into the planning, preparation, and serving of the food and then the cleanup makes being the charming hostess lose its appeal.

This is especially true when one remembers the mess that is created by family members who come to Mom and Dad's for a visit and drop everything just inside the door. Boots and shoes come off the moment they step inside. They are not put aside but reside just where they were removed. Then there is the extra stuff, especially in fall and winter: jackets, books, handbags for the ladies (girls), and fourth but not least, the phones and computers. To that mix, add an animal (dog) that likes to tease the cats, and we are have the total of the visit.

Having said all this, I am almost ashamed to put this on paper, as I always encourage family members to come. I love, love, love having them here, especially the wonderful animals. It is a pleasure for me to have time to connect with my children and their wonderful children and animals. Both Howard and I are in heaven when they come and hate to see them leave. That cannot be overstated. So in order to control my deep emotions about the messes, I drive myself nuts cooking and preparing their favorite dishes, including homemade ice cream—peppermint-stick being the most popular.

When it comes to overnight accommodations, the question is

where will everyone settle? The obvious answer is to find a delightful place to house the bulk of the family. That is where the Stone Gate Club comes in. Two or three years ago, we invited our family members to the mountains for Thanksgiving. In order to alleviate my anxiety and to accommodate the growing group (We now include boyfriends and girlfriends), we made reservations for them to stay at the club. They were as excited as we were because in the past, they have all been to the club for dinner. Being able to have one special Thanksgiving dinner together and spend the night was more than a treat for all of us. Understand that we are not only talking about adults here, there were six youngsters involved in this visit.

They all arrived on the evening before the holiday. At our house, we had a simple supper made up of their favorite casserole, a tossed salad, and fresh biscuits. This was topped off with a scoop of homemade peppermint-stick ice cream. They helped with the cleanup and then departed for the club.

On the phone with Howard and me when they were ready for bed, they told us that upon arriving at the club, they were greeted by a staff member and were shown their accommodations on the second floor. The family settled down after chatting and joking. Our family members had been split up and sent to their bedrooms. Our son Jack and his son Sean occupied one room. Cheryl, our daughter-in-law, and their youngest girl, Kelly, were in the second room. Their older daughters, Louise and Dana, shared another room. Our daughter Nel, her husband Gary, and their two children, Joshua and Perry, occupied another two rooms.

Unbeknownst to the rest of the family, the youngest member, a bright, charming young lady of ten named Kelly, left her room and went downstairs to the gentlemen's library. She was intent on finding something she could read to help her fall sleep. In that room, portraits of past club presidents adorn some of the wall space, as well as hunt scenes.

I guess that because of her imagination, she looked at the portraits and suddenly thought that she saw eyes following her throughout the room. In a *panic*, she dashed out of the room and ran up the stairs to find her family. She was in hysterics.

We were told her older brother Sean, who was always ready to tease her and make her life miserable, had also been headed downstairs to investigate those rooms, which he had spotted when they had first arrived. He saw Kelly looking like a scared rabbit. She told him what had just happened. Sean laughed and called her a sissy and a scaredy-cat. He made such fun of her panic that she was ready to do him some bodily harm.

Just in time, their father, Jack, came out of his bedroom. Realizing the situation could become a major war, he separated the two and made them sit on the sofa in the upper hallway to cool off. Then he insisted that they follow him back downstairs to the library. He would solve the following-eye issue.

Oh, Yea, Dad to the rescue! I thought as he related the story. However, that was one time when dear-ole dad, Jack just didn't have any clout. When they entered the library, one of the portraits lay on the floor. It looked like someone had removed it from the wall and then had put it down on the rug.

Upon seeing the framed piece on the rug, Jack picked it up to rehang it, making sure that no damage had been done. He then turned to Kelly with a questioning look on his face. She nodded her head as if to say yes. That painting had frightened her. Jack accomplished the task of rehanging it while the children watched.

Young Kelly spoke up and said, "Dad, please look at his eyes."

"Yes?" questioned Jack. "What do you expect me to see?"

She looked around and said quietly, "I thought he was following me with his eyes. I was scared to death. But I don't think he'll do that to you. He just does it to kids to scare them."

With that, Jack walked over to the picture and looked at the eyes of the gentleman who was imprisoned in the frame. As he did so, the picture swung, and then it started to fall once again. Jack grabbed it just in time. *What on earth?* he thought. *Surely the hook must not be strong enough to hold the artwork. But that makes no sense. The portrait has hung in the same place for years.*

Meanwhile, Sean was looking around the room. He noticed the fireplace and the ashes that were quietly blowing out of it. Then he started toward the bookcases on other side of the room and saw movement on one of the shelves. He thought he saw something like a small rodent scamper from behind the row of books. When he looked again, he saw nothing but a little stuffed bunny. He thought that it must have been his imagination. It was a story that he would never tell Kelly.

The trip to the gentlemen's library was an unsolved mystery. Jack rounded up the two youngsters and reminded them that it was way past their bedtimes. The puzzle would not be solved that night. "Let's just get some sleep, and we can go over the whole event tomorrow at breakfast," he said.

Thanksgiving morning dawned. Breakfast was served in the downstairs' café. Kelly and Sean avoided the gentlemen's library like the plague, but Jack was curious. He wondered if the portrait had fallen again. So he made a detour and entered the library. The portrait was in place, the ashes were gone, and there was no sign of any furry fellow on the bookcase. *It must have been a figment of our imaginations*, Jack thought.

When he joined his family members, who were eating their delicious breakfast, he told the children what he had seen in the gentlemen's library. They seemed skeptical but didn't argue the facts.

Rory the waiter came to pour more coffee and make sure the guests were happy with their food. He noticed that the children were a bit down in the mouth and almost too quiet. He decided to ask a few questions. "How did you enjoy your rooms last night?" he asked them. There was a moment of silence. "Tell me, did you get a chance to be greeted by our resident ghost?" he asked.

The table erupted. Jack, Kelly, and Sean looked like they were going to burst. "The g-g-ghost does live here?" they asked in unison. "There really is a ghost at Stone Gate?"

Rory smiled and said, "Of course. It is the best person around here. Why, I remember the first time the ghost came to me. I was carrying a tray of empty glasses back to the kitchen when I almost fell. I must have slipped on someone's napkin, which had been dropped on the floor, and didn't see it because of the tray I was carrying.

"From behind me, I felt a hand reach for the tray. I turned around to thank the guy who had saved me from falling and the tray from dumping all those glasses on the floor. There was no one there. No one was anywhere in the room. I was astonished. Then I remembered the story of the ghost who lives here and knew the ghost had helped me."

Now everyone at the table was so quiet you could hear a pin drop. Jack and his two worried children took deep breaths and slowly relaxed. The two oldest girls, Dana and Louise, had slept through the previous night's adventure. Cheryl was surprised when she learned the story of the previous night. She questioned the three of them: Jack, Kelly, and Sean.

There was no reason to believe that a ghost had rescued Rory, recovered the portrait, blown ashes out of the fireplace, or placed a pretend animal on a shelf in the gentlemen's library. However, there had not been any evidence to prove that it had not been a ghost. If the incidents that had happened were indeed true, how could one prove that there was a ghost? It was a quandary.

Rory had moved on to help another table of guests. As he moved amongst the tables and guests, he could feel the tension from the guests who had met the ghost of the Stone Gate Club. He was a bit put off by their attitudes. He felt that they really didn't want to believe in the ghost and that they were being a bit smug. He decided to prove to them that the Stone Gate Club ghost was real. He would make them eat crow by making the real ghost appear. Then they would know for sure that they were not only dreaming.

Breakfast was over. The family retired to their upstairs rooms. A formal dinner was to be served at 1:00 p.m. It was early enough in the day that much could be seen and done before the dinner hour.

Jack packed the family into his new SUV and headed to our home, which was located on the side of Knox Mountain. As they approached our house, he saw a huge eagle flying over it. Eagles are very rare in our mountains, although it isn't unheard of.

Jack told us that he had been so excited to see such a magnificent bird that he had almost missed our driveway. He had slowed so that he could watch the bird and draw his family's attention to the antics of the eagle. The eagle had suddenly swerved, and while flapping its wings, it had landed on the running board of the SUV next to the door on the driver's side. Jack had been thrilled. As the car had approached our house, the eagle had decided to climb onto the roof of the vehicle.

Howard and I were on our porch awaiting the family's arrival. When we saw the vehicle coming up from the valley with an eagle on its roof, we were astounded. Our family members who had stayed at the Stone Gate Club overnight were in the back seat of the SUV as the bird made cackling noises and tried to bombard us as if he had a beak full of ammunition. The kids tried to shoo the bird away but finally gave up. The eagle was not going to leave.

They had a little conference and decided it would be best to accommodate the bird and give it the space it wanted so that we could enjoy its time with us. The eagle moved around the roof of the car screeching. It tried to stop the vehicle from going forward. None of us could believe the scene that was happening before our very eyes. The eagle in all its magnificence was trying to tell us something important, but what? The eagle took off with a great flapping of its wings. We all seemed amazed to see it leave, but realizing that the dinner hour was fast approaching, they all got out of the SUV, hugged and kissed us, and then went inside to say hello to the dogs.

Our two delicious little pugs were the delight of our lives. Howard and I had adopted them from a rescue farm in Alabama a year earlier. We had given them the love and care that they had needed so that they could recover from the terrible conditions they had been found in—starving in a dirty, hot, and moldy kennel where they had been born. Monty and Mika loved the family's attention.

We soon scooted the family out of the house and sent them back to the club to get ready for our Thanksgiving dinner. We then went upstairs to change into our outfits for the occasion.

A terrific time was had by all as we helped ourselves to the grand buffet, which Cliff had set out for us. Not only did we have turkey, but we also had six other delicious dishes. All of them had the taste of the season cooked or baked inside. Then there was the salad table, where we chose from an assortment of three different greens, veggies, cheeses, and dressings. As we completed our main courses, we visited the dessert table. We felt very spoiled by our delightful chef, Cliff, when we spied the table full of wonderful desserts. We wondered where we would put it all.

Saturday rolled around, and the family wanted to gather at our house for another wonderful meal and to just talk. The bulk of the group had spent the day investigating some of the venues that were popular in the mountains. Others—mostly the ladies—found the prime outlet stores in Pennyton, worked on completing their Christmas gift lists, and visited their favorite discount stores.

Too much of everything had been on the schedule. Everyone was tired and wanted to relax and enjoy the last few days in the mountains, but the eagle persisted. It flew around the club, all of Knox, and then our street. It was attracting photographers from all over the county. Once a quiet neighborhood, our street had suddenly been transformed into a destination.

Howard, our neighbors, and I were furious at the traffic and the rudeness of those who came to take photos of the great bird. We stood guard outside of our home on the hill, trying to keep everything neat and clean. We picked up cans, bottles, and plastic drinking cups, to say nothing of the napkins, plastic bags, and other pieces of garbage. Putting up signs didn't do the trick. We finally decided to hire a person to monitor the traffic and to make sure each carload of people removed its own junk.

The weekend flew by. Then it was Monday, and everyone was moaning from enjoying too much good food from the Thanksgiving dinner at the Stone Gate Club and then the leftover dinner the next night.

Meanwhile, the bird was having a wonderful time, soaring all around the property, cackling, every now and then settling on a branch of the huge pine tree, stopping in the driveway, and walking around screeching at the top of its lungs. We were all trying to figure out what the bird was attempting to tell us. In desperation, Howard called the local bird-watchers' society and even the humane society. No one could tell us why this bird was showing off.

My dear darling daughter Nel is so in love with animals that when she was a little girl, she kept us up at night helping her feed those little birdies she would rescue and the litters of kittens, of which she would say, "Oh, Mom, aren't they just dear?" We finally realized that our little girl was an animal lover and that she would never turn her back on any animal in need. She and our daughter-in-law, Cheryl, and our granddaughters had slipped away to Marshalls and T.J. Maxx to shop for winter clothing and Christmas gifts.

I called her on her cell phone. I said, "Nel, please help us figure out why this eagle is bugging us." I filled her in on the story of the ghost at the Stone Gate Club and that it had predicted there would be consequences. Then the eagle had flown into the picture, and someone in the car had asked if it might have been the consequence. She was not impressed.

"But, Nel," I complained, "what are we going to do to keep the bird from bothering us all day long?"

She laughed and said, "Mom, you had better figure out why that wonderful bird has chosen you to bug. I wouldn't be surprised that it has something to do with the Stone Gate Club. Why don't you try to get it to return to the club? Perhaps that will give you some idea as to what is going on with the bird."

"You know," I said, "that is why you are my wonderful daughter. You come up with very logical, concrete ideas when I need them. Thank you, Nel." I rushed out to the driveway. Sure enough, there was the bird. The minute he saw me, he started his incessant cackling. It was enough to drive a sane person insane.

I called Howard to let him know what was taking place and to report on what Nel had said about the eagle. We agreed that we must not let this get us anxious. He recommended that I try to solve the puzzle using Nel's suggestion. I agreed and went to the garage.

As I opened the garage door and backed my car out, the bird immediately flapped his wings and flew into the air. He watched me from above as I turned the car around and drove down the driveway to the street. I spotted the eagle hovering above me and watching my every move. I continued down the street. Once I was on the main road to the Stone Gate Club, I watched as the eagle flew almost overhead.

I drove over the mountain and down into Knox. The eagle followed me every mile. When we reached the turnoff for the club, I watched the bird as it followed me at the turn. He was very tuned into where I was going.

Once I arrived at the entrance to the club, I saw that the eagle was also turning. As I drove to the porch's entrance to the club, a figure, which I had observed many times before, sat there. Each of the other times we had tried, the image had gone before we could approach the porch to identify the person. This time was different. The person sitting on the bench in front of the door to the club stayed there. I tried to see who it was from a distance.

As I parked and alighted from the car, I knew who it was. There was no doubt about it. The person who was waiting on the porch for me to return was none other than our dear friend Rosie Atwater, who had asked us to join the club a few years earlier. Rosie and Lee were special friends.

How wonderful it was to see her during such a stressful time. Surely, she might be able to answer the question about the eagle. If not, we could ask her husband, Lee. Lee and Rosie were members of the local bird-watchers association. The eagle was flying overhead. It acted so excited that I hoped it would not keel over in flight and fall to the ground, but it didn't. As it flapped its wings and chirped as a happy bird does, it flew all around the porch and the lawn of the club.

Members who were playing croquet on the grass next to the clubhouse were agog at the antics of this beautiful bird. Then it disappeared. I thought I saw it off in the distance, but I couldn't be sure.

That evening as a number of us gathered for cocktails on the club's porch, the subject of the eagle came up. We all asked where the bird had disappeared to. Thus the events of the past few days became the main topic of conversation. It was very quietly concluded that a ghost must have been contributing to the mystique of the club. As for the eagle, it had just taken a liking to the top of the car, which shined like a mirror. It had come out of the woods and had been looking for a place to land and to get a drink of water. It was suggested that the eagle thought the roof of the car looked like a small pond, and hence, it began its flight with us.

CHAPTER 11

BEFORE THE BEGINNING

Ghosts might frighten little people. That was not my intent when I tried to clear up the mystery of a ghost that might have been making itself known. I wanted to make sure that guests of the club, if they were concerned, knew that the ghost was a friendly shadow or someone who would help maintain a happy atmosphere at the Stone Gate Club. It surely had not been to frighten anyone.

Most of the guests had no idea that there were ghosts that might frighten their families. Most of the guests came to enjoy the ambiance of the local area: Snaglewood, Shakespeare Theatre's productions, the Mountain Theatre Festival, and so forth. Some of the guests came to enjoy the croquet fields and the tennis courts or just to relax in an atmosphere of friendliness, as they had done for many years.

To even suggest that there was a ghost among them was almost an insult. Hence, when the stories began to appear about a sighting of a ghost at the club, those guests who had made a yearly visit to this part of the mountains were just a bit miffed.

"That's ridiculous," said Tony Major, one of the guests from New Hampshire who had been returning the longest. We had met the Majors as they had arrived for their yearly participation in the kickoff of the croquet season. Tony came each year to participate in the croquet tournaments. For nigh on twenty years, he had been a nonresident member of the Stone Gate Club. Each year, he had brought his wife, Ellen. If he could coax their two children to join them, Stanley and Irene would also participate in the tournaments.

This year, however, Tony was unable to get their grown children to come with them for the week of tournament fun. Monday morning, Tony and Ellen, who were outfitted in their regulation croquet garb, arrived at the croquet courts ready to do battle with other entrants in the tournament. Breezy and Louise Paine of Dorchester, Massachusetts, Richard and Judith Keating of Brattleboro, Vermont, and Dr. and Mrs. (Simon and Sophia) Sunderland of Boylston, Massachusetts, were all there awaiting the drop of the ball. But where was the ball?

In great frustration and shouldering his mallet, Tony looked everywhere for the ball, which would signify the beginning of the tournament. He was annoyed. He wondered why the club didn't take the time to make sure the ball was available for the beginning of that year's very important tournament. He was more than relieved to see the ball come rolling down the hill from the clubhouse toward him. That was unusual. Usually balls were in place in front of the wickets.

The tournament got underway. Tony moved the ball toward the hoop and hit it through without a problem. Then everything seemed to go awry. The ball disappeared. In frustration, Tony walked across the court to where he had seen the ball disappear. There was no sign of any ball. When he turned around, he was astounded to see the ball back at the spot where he had last seen it. It was ready for his swing into action.

It was as if the ball had a mind of its own. It would be ready to be hit and then would move on without being hit across the court to the next hoop. Once the person who was to hit the ball next appeared, the ball would suddenly move in another direction. This caused chaos among the players.

I asked the judge, Tom Bickery, for an intermission. The ball was picked up and inspected by the judge. There seemed to be no problem with the equipment. So what was causing the ball to act so queerly?

Little Allen Rich, one of the newer member's sons, was at the club during all of this craziness on the croquet courts. Allen, who as ten years old, was a handsome and intelligent youngster with a vivid imagination and great inquisitiveness. He overheard us talking on the about the crazy actions of the ball. He decided to investigate the reasons for the ball's misbehavior.

Allen slowly scooted down the lawn between the croquet and tennis courts, watching for anything that might tell him what was going on. As he approached the second croquet court, he thought he saw a small movement in the grass at the left side of the court. As he watched and walked slowly toward the movement, he realized that he was seeing a small figure holding a croquet ball in its hands.

Approaching the figure, Allen began to ask a question. The figure disappeared. Allen was surprised. He decided to continue to where the figure had been. The ball was there, but no one was with it. Allen picked up the ball, and it was immediately pushed out of his hands. The ball rolled down the side of the court and landed at the beginning of the hoops. Allen followed the ball.

Junior Malady was just about ready to hit the ball through the first hoop when Allen appeared behind the ball. The ball aimed itself at the hoop and went through it and across the lawn to the next hoop. Allen looked bewildered but no more than Junior did. They both wondered what had happened to the ball.

It suddenly came to rest at the hoop and didn't seem to want to move. Junior followed the ball to the hoop. He tried to hit the ball. It would not have any of it but rolled through the hoop without any indication of having been hit through by Junior.

Spectators who were interested in the tournament watched the antics of the ball. When it went through the hoop without a hit from Junior, the observers howled and began clapping. Junior was stunned. He wondered what he should do now. What would the judge say about the score?

Before anyone could comment on it, the ball went flying back to the beginning hoop. There it stayed, seeming to wait for someone to hit it through the first hoop.

The judge climbed down from his perch and walked across the court to examine the ball himself. As he got closer, the ball started to wiggle. It wiggled and wiggled until the spectators began to laugh. The ball was being crazy.

We all watched, including little Betsy Boudreau, the youngest daughter of Mike and Julie Boudreau, who were on the tennis court for their match with Mary Alice and Ron Rich. Betsy stood in a corner of the clubhouse. While her mom and dad played tennis, she watched the antics on the croquet court unfold.

Suddenly, she realized that she was not alone. When she turned and looked up, she was aware of the pretty face of a young but older girl standing almost next to her.

Betsy said, "I didn't see you come in." The older girl just looked at her and smiled. "My name is Betsy. What's yours?" The girl still didn't answer. Betsy reached out and tried to pull on the sleeve of the girl's sweater. The sleeve and the girl disappeared. Betsy was so upset that she started to cry. She wondered where the girl had gone. She decided to ask someone else if they had seen the girl.

Rory the waiter was setting the table with soft drinks, water, and a few tasty-looking nibbles for the croquet teams. She spotted him and ran up to ask if he had seen the lovely girl. Just as he had recently done, Rory said to her, "You mean the ghost?"

Betsy looked at Rory as if he was crazy. "A g-ghost?" she said. "Do you really think it was a ghost?"

Rory laughed and started to explain when a croquet ball hit his shin. "Ouch!" Rory cried. "Now where did that come from?"

Meanwhile, Betsy was smiling at the lovely girl who had again appeared next to her. The girl just smiled and shook her head. For Betsy, the puzzle was solved. It was a ghost but a lovely, sweet one.

As I arrived on the scene, Betsy told me that she was content with the reason she had found for all the excitement on the croquet court. It had been due to the girl. She filled me in on the events that had taken place just before I had arrived. Betsy shook with laughter, and she was relieved. She said that the ghost of the Stone Gate Club was there for no other purpose than to protect the members and their families and to have fun while doing it.

Incidentally, Tony and Ellen won the tournament. Tony was in high gear when they showed up at the club for dinner that evening. His fellow croquet players feted him and threatened to unseat him during the next year's tournament. It turned out to be a wonderful yearly event at the Stone Gate Club.

CHAPTER 12

THE CLEANUP

At the end of the summer season, the Boston Symphony Orchestra and the Boston Pops performed at Snaglewood. Shakespeare and Family, Dorman Mockwell Museum, and all the other summer events finished their wonderful shows and exhibits for that season. It was time to clean up and get ready for fall and winter in the mountains.

The leaves had begun to fall. The trees were wearing their fall coats, and the mountain ridges shone with vivid color. All the venues began planning their fall events. It was not only Halloween but also harvesttime. Then the Thanksgiving and Christmas holidays and all the wonderful, colorful happenings that surrounded those magical times came. It was truly a great time to be in touch with nature and her garb for the last months of the year in the wonderful mountains of Vermont.

The Stone Gate Club was going at full speed to keep up with the guests and events that were happening daily. Once again, school was in session. Some pupils came to the club for their piano lessons with Joyce Turnbul, the most prominent teacher in town. The little ones would troop up onto the porch and wait on a settee for their lessons with Joyce.

Scouts trooped through the wooded area behind the club and studied ugly little crawly bugs, which they collected and identified so that they could earn a badge in bug life. They usually wanted a campfire, but that was a no-no. Having the troop at the club kept the staff on their toes. They had to watch the young men for signs of any unusual activity.

Zillian Marcourt told me that she had volunteered to give tennis lessons to youngsters whose families were members of the club. I was delighted, as my grandson Perry, who was very much into the tennis scene, was to be with us for an extended visit while his parents went on a longtime-planned trip to Europe.

Zilly was a semipro. She had retired from the tennis circuit due to a serious injury to her left hip. She was able to hit a ball with great accuracy, but she had trouble running to catch a hit and send it over the net from the baseline. She loved her sport, and she was loathe to give it up. So to keep active, she decided to give lessons.

Amanda Bigelow was the bridge expert. She had decided to set up a clinic for those members who wished to improve their skills at the game of bridge. Amanda had played bridge all her life, and she was an expert. Each Tuesday, members who wished to have her help signed up and waited for the club to open.

With all the events happening at the club, we needed extra help to arrange the furniture, set up and take down beverage stations, and clean so that everything worked in the best way possible. Hence, when Mondays rolled around, you might find Jean and George Rand somewhere in the club putting the club back in order after a busy weekend and preparing for the upcoming week's events.

Jean Rand was also in charge of the guest rooms on the second floor. She kept them as shiny clean as possible. She was available if anyone needed extra soap or such.

Jean told me later that she had arrived that Monday morning and had been all set to go to work. Gathering her supplies, she quietly moved up the stairs. As she approached the landing on the second floor, she was startled to see a gentleman in croquet whites leaving the Knox Room, which was room number one. He walked across the hallway and into the Richmond Room, which was room number four. Recently, the bedrooms had been named for towns in the mountains but could still be identified by their numbers.

Jean was so startled that she started to shake. There was no reason to see anyone upstairs in the bedroom areas. She had double-checked with Cliff Johnson, the manager, to make sure she could do her weekly cleaning while no one was in the bedrooms.

So she wondered who the man walking from one room to the other had been. She hadn't recognized him. He hadn't seen her as she had walked up the carpeted stairs without making any noise. She wondered if he was a guest, a ghost, or someone she had dreamed up. The experience left her shaken.

She called down the stairs to her husband, George. George could hear the panic in her voice and quickly ran up the stairs to see if she was all right. She was stuttering about a man who had come out of the Knox Room and had walked across to the Richmond Room.

Jean couldn't get the picture out of her mind. She said that it continued to haunt her each time she walked up the stairs at the Stone Gate Club.

CHAPTER 13

A MAGIC WEDDING

A huge wedding party took up all the bedrooms for the weekend of September 16 and used all the function rooms on the first floor. The bride, Marielle Sommers, worried that the weather might not be very good. But her groom, Toby Hearst, told her that the forecast had said there would only be a slight chance of showers. It turned out to be very pleasant all weekend. That was a bonus for the bridal party and the staff of the Stone Gate Club.

A huge tent was constructed on the grounds in front of the porch. Inside, lights hung from the ceiling throughout the tent. Tables were set with sparkling-white tablecloths and napkins. Centerpieces with white lilies, beautiful hydrangeas, and green leaves set the tone for the wedding event of the season.

A string quartet was in one corner. Speakers were stationed everywhere on the grounds of the club. A long table was set up in front of the guest tables. It sported two massive flower arrangements on each end and space in the center of the table for the bridal cake.

The wedding itself was to be conducted inside the club in the beautiful music room. The service was to be held in front of the fireplace. Many chairs were set up auditorium style for the guests in front of the fireplace, which was at the front of the room. Flower arrangements were placed on the first chairs in each row to match the arrangements on the tables. It looked just like a spectacular wedding should look. Red carpet, which led to the front of the room, set the tone for the wedding.

Marielle and Toby were thrilled when they were given a quick preview before they went upstairs to their separate rooms to get dressed. It was going to be a fantastic celebration of their love for one another.

Once the bridal party was dressed and ready for the wedding ceremony, they descended the main staircase to the clubhouse. The groomsmen followed the groom into the music room. They would be the ushers. The attendants to the bride descended the same main staircase. They waited in the hallway until the music indicated that they were to approach the front of the room where the minister, the groom, and groomsmen stood. They proceeded to walk down the red carpet.

The guests stood and turned around as Marielle hooked her arm through her father's arm and began the walk down the aisle to the fireplace where the groom and company awaited. The ceremony began.

Once the vows had been made, the groom kissed the bride as the guests applauded. Then the couple walked along the same aisle, where only moments before, they had walked as single persons. They now returned as husband and wife.

In the hallway of the club, they stood in a receiving line to welcome their guests, along with their parents and the bridal party. As Howard and I moved up in line, we couldn't help but remember our own wedding, which had taken place over forty years earlier. We spoke with other guests who were waiting to congratulate the couple. The guests were swept up in the memories of their own wedding days.

After the receiving line, the entire entourage moved outside to the tent. The photographer had finished taking all the pictures he could of the receiving line and the guests, as they had flowed through the line with their congratulations.

The guests followed the bridal party into the tent, which was stationed on the croquet court in front of the clubhouse. They were excited for the lovely couple, and they wanted to get as close to them as they could. Crowding up to the newlyweds, they tried to let them know how much they appreciated being a part of their special day.

Marielle and Toby tried to speak with all their friends and family members before heading to their table, which was the table with the lovely flower arrangements and the beautiful wedding cake.

The ringing of bells announced that it was time for the bride and groom to cut their cake. The bride was given a knife to perform that act. However, as Marielle started to make the first cut, the knife slipped out of her hand and fell to the floor. Staff member Jean Rand realized that the knife needed to be washed before it could be used again. She took the knife into the kitchen, washed it, and started back to the tent to give it to the bride. Before she could leave the kitchen, the knife was on the floor again. Jean wasn't sure how that had happened, but she needed to clean it under the faucet again.

As she once again cleaned the knife and started to walk back to the tent, the club manager, Cliff Johnson, came through the back of the kitchen holding up a beautiful silver serving knife, which had been tied with a lovely white satin bow. He exchanged his knife for Jean's knife. It seemed the correct thing to do, as the new knife had been a gift from one of Marielle's best friends, who was also her maid of honor.

The cake was cut and distributed among the guests. There were accolades for the chef who had made the delicious cake. Many guests decided to keep their portions of cake so that they could put them under their pillows that night and request positive things for their lives from the pillow fairy.

That weekend, Jean and George Rand were on hand to help serve drinks and food. Jean watched as the bride and groom arrived at the head table, where their beautiful cake was displayed. After helping with the lovely luncheon, Jean was assigned to help serve the cake.

After the meal was served, the orchestra in the corner began playing the "Wedding Waltz." Marielle and Toby went to the dance floor. The dance lessons they had taken in the last three months paid off in a wonderful display by the bride and groom. Soon all the guests had grabbed partners, and they were trying to outdo the wedding party. They danced until their feet hurt.

Toby led his bride back to the head table. She picked up her lovely bridal bouquet and gathered her bridal party together. The entourage left the tent's dance floor and went to the porch.

Marielle stood on the porch while her attendants and other single ladies stood just outside of the tent on the croquet court. Marielle turned away from her girlfriends. She then raised her arm and counted to three. Then she tossed the bridal bouquet over her head and back to Sheila LaPointe, her maid of honor and best friend from college. Sheila was so excited that she almost cried.

Her fiancé, Ben Whittle, was standing on the porch waiting for her. When he saw Sheila catch the flowers, he was delighted. Their relationship had been rocky for the first few months, but it had soon become evident that love was in the air when Ben had realized what a treasure he had in this beauty. He had proposed the week before the Hearst wedding. Now they could get serious about their own wedding plans. He could hardly wait to discuss those plans with Sheila.

As afternoon was moving into evening, the clouds that Marielle had worried about earlier began to dissipate. The warm autumn air became a bit brisk.

Marielle went upstairs to the room in the club, which had been provided for the bridal party. She made a quick change into her traveling clothes. When her maid of honor signaled Marielle, she appeared in the upstairs hallway and met her new husband, Toby. He escorted her down the stairs and into the library.

Once there, the photographer, Casey Jones, was ready to take his final pictures of the wedding party. Sheila and Ben with their moms and dads from both sides of the wedding party gathered in front of the fireplace in that auspicious room. Marielle and Toby were holding hands and standing in the middle of the group.

The flash exploded. Something was wrong with the camera. It fell to the floor. When Casey tried to pick it up, the camera rolled to the door, and then it became caught on a corner of the rug. Casey tried to pick it up, but the camera had a mind of its own. It somehow was wrenched away from Casey, and it disappeared.

Now this was not funny. The bride and groom were upset. The groom tried to calm his new wife, but she was so frightened that he had a real case on his hands. Finally, he was able to calm her and himself.

As all the wedding pictures were on the film in that camera, the entire group was going a bit crazy. Mom and Dad Sommers were especially concerned about their daughter, the bride. They wondered what had happened, why it had happened, and where the camera had gone. Was it still in the club? The answer to the question as to where the camera went was up in the air.

Casey was developing a severe case of anxiety. He wondered what had happened to his precious new camera. It was state-of-the-art equipment for wedding photographers. He had his reputation to uphold. He needed to find that camera.

He had to scour the entire premises. He would start right where he was standing. He would proceed to the areas inside the club and then to the tent where the reception was held. But he had better hurry because the bridal party was leaving soon, and he wanted to take pictures of their departure.

There was no sign of the camera anywhere in the clubhouse. Casey enlisted any staff that was not busy cleaning up to help him locate the camera. The grounds were next. As Casey started to hunt outside the clubhouse and near the parking lot, he saw his car. Casey decided to put the camera bag and some of the equipment into his car. Casey opened the door to the trunk, put his equipment in, and then shut the door. He turned to look inside the car, and lo and behold, he saw in amazement that the camera was there. It was sitting on the front seat of his SUV. Hooray, it was found!

This was a wonderful ending to a beautiful day. We watched the bride and groom amidst the shower of rice that was being tossed at them as they climbed into their limousine. Then they left the club, and they were on their way to their honeymoon.

The staff was pleased with how the event had come together. The parents were delighted that the wedding was over and that they could go home and rest. The guests were happy to have had a chance to be with their friends and to do a bit of dancing down memory lane, as they remembered the time that they had walked down the aisle to get married.

All in all, it was a very delightful event. Howard and I were sure that the ghost of the Stone Gate Club had even enjoyed it. As the club closed, the lights were turned off, the parking lot was emptied, and the winds blew, the ghost of the club could once again settle down, have an undisturbed rest, and contemplate the events of the past year. At least, that's what we thought the ghost might do …